ALL THE
TRUTH
THAT'S IN
ME

ALL THE
TRUTH
THAT'S IN
ME

JULIE BERRY

VIKING

An Imprint of Penguin Group (USA) Inc.

VIKING
Published by the Penguin Group
Penguin Group (USA) Inc.
375 Hudson Street
New York, New York 10014, U.S.A.

Ⓟ

USA / Canada / UK / Ireland / Australia / New Zealand /
India / South Africa / China
Penguin Books Ltd, Registered Offices:
80 Strand, London WC2R 0RL, England

For more information about the Penguin Group visit
www.penguin.com

First published in the United States of America by Viking,
an imprint of Penguin Group (USA) Inc., 2013

Translation of Ovid's *Metamorphoses* by Julie Berry.

LIBRARY OF CONGRESS CATALOGING-IN-PUBLICATION DATA
Berry, Julie, date.
All the truth that's in me / by Julie Berry.
pages cm
Summary: "Judith can't speak. But when her close-knit community of
Roswell Station is attacked by enemies, Judith is forced to choose: continue
to live in silence, or recover her voice"
—Provided by publisher.
ISBN 978-0-670-78615-2 (hardcover : alk. paper) [1. Selective mutism—
Fiction. 2. Community life—Fiction. 3. War—Fiction.]
I. Title. II. Title: All the truth that's in me.
PZ7.B461747Al 2013
[Fic]—dc23
2012043218

Printed in USA

3 5 7 9 10 8 6 4 2

Designed by Eileen Savage
Set in Sabon

For Phil

The mouth of the just bringeth forth wisdom: but the froward
tongue shall be cut out.

Proverbs 10:31

ALL THE
TRUTH
THAT'S IN
ME

Before

We came here by ship, you and I.

I was a baby on my mother's knee, and you were a lisping, curly-headed boy playing at your mother's feet all through that weary voyage.

Watching us, our mothers got on so well together that our fathers chose adjacent farm plots a mile from town, on the western fringe of a Roswell Station that was much smaller then.

I remember my mother telling tales of the trip when I was young. Now she never speaks of it at all.

She said I spent the whole trip wide-eyed, watching you.

After

BOOK ONE

I.

You didn't come.

I waited all evening in the willow tree, with gnats buzzing in my face and sap sticking in my hair, watching for you to return from town.

I know you went to town tonight. I heard you ask Mr. Johnson after church if you could pay a call on him this evening. You must want to borrow his ox team.

But you were gone so long. You never came. Maybe they asked you to supper. Or maybe you went home another way.

Mother chided me ragged for missing chores and supper, and said all that was left for me was what had stuck to the stew pot. Darrel had already scraped the pot bare, but Mother made me wash it in the stream anyway.

There's nothing so bright as the stream by day, nothing so black on a moonless night.

I bent and drank straight from it. It was all I had to fill my belly. And maybe, I thought, you'd be thirsty, too, after a scratchy day of haying, and before retiring to bed you'd dip down into the same stream and drink the water I had kissed. You've cooled off here most summer nights since you were a boy.

I thought how, in the darkness, I would feel like any other girl to you. Beneath my dress I have no cause for shame.

I thought how, if you knew, you might look twice at me, bend your thoughts my way and see if they snap quickly back, or linger.

But you don't know.

And you never will.

For I am forbidden from telling.

II.

This morning I was in the fringe of woods beyond your cabin long before you were up. I had to circle around a tree so you wouldn't see me when you passed by on your way to the outhouse.

Something occupies your thoughts today. There's a spring in your step, and you hum as you walk. You seem in a hurry to get on with something.

Jip didn't notice me. He hovered at your ankles and rubbed his side against your boot. He's half deaf and blind, with little left of his sense of smell, but still you keep him. He's an old friend.

I watched your cabin as long as I could before I had to hurry back, lest Mother notice me missing.

III.

Darrel knows. He caught me in the woods outside your house. He threatens to tell Mother, if I don't do his chores for him in the chicken hut and bring him berries and nuts and first cherries whenever I find them. He and his great mouth need my constant feeding in order to stop their constant talking.

IV.

Tonight the moon came out, and I went out with it, to watch it rise over the treetops. So silent, the moon.

I remember. Night after night, its silence would comfort me. How dark the nights when it went away. But it always came back.

It was my only friend in the years with him.

It is still my consolation.

V.

You are not like him.

No matter what anyone says.

VI.

Father used to say my singing could charm the birds down from the trees. Loving fathers will say anything, but I used to dream one day my song would bring you to me.

It was always you. When you gathered nuts in the forest with the other coltish boys, I liked your smiles and jokes the best. I swelled with pride when your slingshot brought down a big tom turkey.

Do you remember me digging worms for you when you were twelve and I was eight?

I would meet you at the creek with my little sack of soil and present you with the fattest crawlers I could pluck from pulling weeds in my mother's kitchen garden. You called me "Ladybird." It was Father's name for me. He meant "sweetheart." You meant "girl worm-catcher." I was still pleased.

You'd do somersaults when you knew that only I could see

them. You pretended not to hear me clapping, and we'd both laugh when you toppled on your rear.

You left a basket of apples for me at my willow tree once. I saw you sneak away after.

In time, you became a man, and all at once, I became this.

VII.

Do you remember the Aldruses' logrolling? I can never forget it, though I suppose it must be just another day to you.

It was four years ago. I was just fourteen, and growing.

It was a hot day in late summer. A young couple had recently arrived in Roswell Station from Newkirk, up north, and they wanted to set up housekeeping east of town, where the last forest overlooks the marshlands. Clyde Aldrus had staked out a lot and asked the town to come clear away the timber he'd felled. His young wife, Joan, was near to delivering her first.

You must remember the day's work. You left your ripening wheat fields and toiled under the hot sun all day with your hatchet and ax, in company with the men and older boys and the oxen and their chains.

But do you remember the food? And what you said to the girl who prepared and served the hominy pudding?

I hope you do not remember my hominy pudding. I would rather forget that. I chose it because I'd heard you say once, after church, that it was one of your favorite suppers.

Our whole family came: Mother, Father, Darrel, and me. Father whistled all the way through town, driving Old Ben hitched to our apple cart. Mother sat beside him and shook her head, laughing at him. I held on tight to the hominy pudding cradled in my lap.

Mother sat with the women and sewed gowns and bonnets for the new baby. The young ladies presided over the table in their absence. We were all so nervous, we girls, about presenting our cooking to Roswell Station for the first time.

I stood slicing pears with Abigail Pawling when someone tugged me aside.

"Can you keep a secret?" Lottie Pratt whispered under her bonnet brim into my ear.

"Of course I can," I said. "What's the matter?"

She led me behind the pile of logs already gathered by sweating men. Back at the table, Maria Johnson and Eunice Robinson eyed us. Maria's new dress was blood red, with a white scalloped collar and black ribbons on the sleeves and bodice. Earlier, when Maria was out of hearing, little Elizabeth Frye said her father thought the dress dipped dangerously close to vanity. And if beauty wasn't enough, while the rest of us girls struggled with our puddings and hotchpots, Maria Johnson had brought three golden-brown plum tarts.

Lottie, who'd done all her father's cooking since her mother's death many years ago, had no reason to fear being outshone by Maria. Her yeasty rolls could rival even Goody Pruett's baking. She pulled my ear close to her mouth.

"I've got a fella," she whispered.

I pulled away to see her face. She must be joking. But her cheeks were flushed, and her eyes were bright.

"Who?" I breathed.

"Sssh! Tell you later," she said. "Watch me tonight and guess. But swear you'll never speak a word of it."

My head spun with this information. From the corner of my eye, I saw you fasten a chain around a log and wave to Leon Cartwright, who led the ox team.

"What do you *mean*, you've got a fella?"

Lottie's chest swelled with her importance. "Says he's gonna marry me," she said. "He's given me ever so many kisses."

"Kisses!" I gasped. Lottie pressed her pink finger over my lips.

You turned then and saw us whispering there, and straightened up and grinned. I had to take a deep breath.

Lottie missed nothing. Her eyebrows rose. In a terrible instant I realized: you might be her fella.

"Is it Lucas, Lottie?"

She giggled. "What if it is?"

Eunice and Maria were openly frowning at us now. Mrs. Johnson approached the food table, and Maria pointed her mother's gaze our way.

"I've got to know," I begged.

"Why, is Lucas *your* fella?"

I prayed my weakness wouldn't show. "Don't tease me, Lottie," I said. "Just tell me."

A shadow passed over us both, and we looked up to see Mrs. Johnson's arms folded across her ample bosom. "Hadn't you young ladies best get back to your tasks?" she said.

Lottie hurried off, but I trotted meekly back to the table.

"There's a good girl," Mrs. Johnson said, and patted my back. "Lads'll want food soon, and you'll want to show off your pretty face *and* your pretty dish."

I turned to Mrs. Johnson in much astonishment, but she only winked back. Her daughter, Maria, was less patient with me.

"Run and fill these from the well." She handed me two large tin pitchers. I didn't mind an excuse to step away, so I headed toward the new well Clyde had dug.

I dropped the bucket down and listened to it splash. When I was sure it had sunk deep enough to fill, I leaned all my weight against the crank to pull it up again. This pulley was more stubborn than some, and I struggled to complete each turn.

"Let me help," said a voice. Someone beside me took hold of the crank.

It was you.

I wanted to run, but I had pitchers to fill, and how would that look if I bolted away? I hesitated with my hands still on the wooden handle, and you smiled at me.

"Here, we'll do it together," you said. With your hands overlapping mine, you rotated the well-pull effortlessly. My arms followed the motions to no useful purpose. I was sure my cheeks must have gone cherry red. You were almost a man now. It had happened to you so suddenly.

You brought up the bucket and poured water into my pitchers. Then you offered me a cold drink from the cup hooked to the bucket rim, and there was your boy smile in a broader, more angular face. I was so nervous, my arms shook to hold the pitchers. You took one of them and carried it back with me to the table.

"You've grown taller, Ladybird."

"That's what Mother says," I managed to say. "She's had to make me a new dress to fit."

I wanted to die of shame. Mentioning the fit of my dress to any young man, and worse, to you!

I floundered for rescue. "She . . . made me do a great deal of the stitching myself."

You glanced sideways at my gray dress, then up at me. "Looks like you've made a handy job of it."

We reached the table and set the water down. Maria Johnson saw you and twined her bonnet strings between her thumb and finger.

"Dinner's not for an hour yet, Mr. Whiting, so you'll have to come back then," she said. "We can see you're working up an appetite."

Your gaze lingered on Maria's dark curls poking out from under her starched white bonnet. Then you tipped your broad hat at all the girls and strode off to the log-pull. Maria and Eunice both watched you go. I let out a long breath and leaned against the rough-hewn wall of the Aldruses' new home. Lottie caught my eye and smiled, and I sighed in great relief.

I knew then that you were not her fella.

That was the last conversation you and I had, and the last time I saw Lottie smile.

VIII.

The first red leaves appear on the maples. The morning air is cool.

I sit in the willow's branches and watch the chipmunks hard at work. A squirrel on a limb just above scolds me, showing teeth. He waits as if he expects an answer.

Golden light flickers through the pale leaves. In every bit of beauty, I see you.

You have your mother's face. Your father's strength, but your mother's face, made masculine and brown.

I remember her. So pretty, she made young girls jealous. So gentle, old women scolded her for it. So lonely, she succumbed to the dark-haired traveler your family boarded for a fortnight, and followed him on his journey west.

Reverend Frye preached the seventh commandment for half a year after that.

Reverend Frye never could take his eyes off her, either.

IX.

You miss your mother. Her loss made you older overnight, and the lines have never left your face.

There was one who took her leaving worse, and he is your greater tragedy.

X.

He never felt like your father to me. I knew he was, of course, yet never believed it. I never saw the cords of blood binding his flesh to yours. There were only cords of madness strangling him.

Your father died the night the town believed he did, and my captor was born from his ashes. Two men, not alike, strangers to each other.

XI.

The morning after the logrolling, I found something tucked

in a wedge of branches in my willow tree. It was a bunch of posies, tied together with a wheat straw.

I ran home with them, brimming with delicious hope, imagining you in every kind of girlish dream.

I knew exactly what those flowers meant to you.

They weren't the first posies you'd brought me there.

I tried to imagine what I'd do when I saw you next, what I wouldn't say, and would; how I'd let you know without saying so that I cherished your gift.

Two years would pass before I'd get my chance, and by then, there was nothing left to say.

XII.

Lookout duty is yours tonight, so your bed will lie cold while you sit in a cabin perched on a hillside miles away and watch the sea. Clouds and storms you'll see, for the ocean is a restless neighbor, but it is the threat of lights by night and sails by day that takes farmers from their fields and beds. The homelanders will not forget the welcome we gave their first expedition when their ships found our river, and they looked upon our farms with lustful eyes. Long years we've braced ourselves for their angry retribution.

I'll sleep poorly knowing you're so far down the track and suffering to stay awake.

This is the silent price of vigilance.

At least you'll have Jip to keep you company.

XIII.

Darrel will have no more of schooling, he said when he came home this afternoon. The new schoolmaster's tedious, and he's introducing Latin. What use is Latin? If English is good enough for the Bible, it's good enough for Darrel. So reasons my brother, the philosopher, and he cracks his slate over the hearth to clinch his argument.

Man of the house, he calls himself! The orator dreams of soldiering. He takes Father's pistol to train his aim on rabbits. The rabbits need not fear, but Darrel would fear for his own hide if he had any sense.

Father wouldn't have stood for Darrel leaving school— and Darrel head of his class, no less!—but Father isn't here anymore, and Mother needs an extra hand at harvesting.

Father wouldn't have liked to see us earn our living brewing spirits, either.

XIV.

I kneel in the garden to pull the beets. They burst free on the first tug, fat and voluptuous, and my basket soon fills. I shake the beets in clumps and dirt rains down.

Father loved this soil. Mother was the only thing he loved more, and he loved her fiercely. He made this farm fruitful and beautiful. While he lived, few farmers in Roswell Station were as admired.

I feel closest to my father when my arms are caked with good brown earth. And so I stay to help my mother, as he would want me to.

XV.

You were not in search of an ox team when you sought to visit Mr. Johnson. You had a deeper favor to ask.

I heard Maria talking to Eunice Robinson at the well on

the green. They all forget that I have ears. Or they don't care.

Maria boasts, but her eyes don't.

You will marry her at the next full moon.

XVI.

Are you proud to wed the village prize? Satisfied to beat out Leon Cartwright and Jud Mathis?

Do you do this for love, or money? To erase the stain of your father's fall?

Or to be rid of me?

XVII.

I flee to my rock in the woods, the place where Father and I would go to sing. I watch the sun set, the slim moon rise and fall.

Mother will murder me.

You are to marry.

Night is cold, like the river, who beckons me with her song.

I came back from two years with him as if from the grave, to a new day among the living, and thought myself happy to return. But the night and the cold, the dark and dead feel more like home to me now.

Only the thought of you dispels my darkness. You are the sun in my world, and how can I endure to watch you set into another woman's arms?

XVIII.

Come morning, I enter the house and Mother slaps me so hard even Darrel pities me.

"You of all people should know better than this," she says.

"After all the sleepless nights you gave me before! You've got no proper feelings!"

XIX.

I rake the coop and gather the eggs, milk the cow, and dump the ashes. Water from the stream, and wood from the pile, then I wash up and wheel the cart to town.

Deliveries done at last, I run to my willow.

There was never a hope. I'm entitled to nothing. There is no one to tell, and no way to tell it, as I am now. I couldn't find words even if I was able. No words could ease this unbearable weight.

I cry to my willow tree: robbed of years, robbed of dignity, language, tranquillity.

Last of all, cruelest, robbed of you.

XX.

Housewives and daughters, like chattering squirrels, revel in news: a wedding soon! The bride, so beautiful, the groom so tall, the pick of the village. Their marriage will be a festival day. Maria's relations will steal daylight to crochet her laces.

All the other little broken hearts—and there are bound to be many—will burn on the altar to youthful beauty and love. It's thin comfort to think I'm not alone in my woe.

XXI.

The sun still rises; roosters still crow and the cow still makes mud. Dunging out her stall was once Darrel's job. Nothing like fresh manure to season a heartache and show me what my fancies are worth.

Uptown, during errands, I see you on the street, surrounded by well-wishers who heap their congratulations on you. A few men harangue you with jokes. Your smiling face is apple red.

Standing near me are some who whisper about your father's slide into his pit of drink. They whisper that you'll do the same, but whisper only. When you approach, they smile and clap your back and say, What a fine farm, Lucas. What a fine wife she'll be, Lucas. You've got a man's shoulders now, Lucas. Just like—

They stop, they stammer. They remember some other errand.

For all they know of your father, they should pity him. They should mourn.

Only one person knows a reason to fear him.

And she has no daggers in her tongue for you.

XXII.

There is much I don't remember.

Sometimes in my dreams the memories return and I cry out. Or I wake and feel caged by the darkness, and forget I'm no longer with him.

Mother yanks my hair then, and orders me to stop my devilish wailing.

XXIII.

Today I took Mother's basket of eggs and a jug of cider into town. Walking toward Abe Duddy's shop, I saw Leon Cartwright cross the street to catch Maria. She was on her way somewhere, and from the looks of it, couldn't get there fast enough. I was only ten paces behind them, but neither of them heeded me.

"Marry him, will you," says he, right in her face.

"I'll marry him if I choose to," says she, walking on as if he's not there, so fast he has to trot to keep up with her.

"You don't love him," says he.

She stops. "I'll love him if I choose to."

"Pah."

She walks again. He grabs her arm. "You only want his farm," he says. "He'll never have your heart."

That's when I took an egg from my basket and whipped it as hard as I could at Leon. The shell smashed, and the yolk soaked into his curly head.

He turned, shouting, then saw that it was me. That made him stop. Years ago it wouldn't have.

I glared at him. He plucked the shells from his hair and cursed but did nothing more.

Maria regarded me. Those dark eyes that drive you wild looked me up and down as though she was seeing me for the first time. She almost smiled. She almost nodded. Then she turned and walked on, leaving Leon to go home and dunk his head.

XXIV.

I realized how easy it would have been to miss and hit her with my egg instead.

I wondered if that was what I should have done.

XXV.

Tobias Salt, the miller's freckle-faced son, trudges back into town from a long night's lookout. His eyes are puffy and his footsteps slow.

"See anything, Toby?" Abe Duddy calls from his shop.

"Never do," says Tobias, and he rubs his eyes.

"That's what I call a good watch," says the old store-keeper.

XXVI.

How busy you are now. Harvest, and a wedding. A new room on the cabin to please your bride. Timber to cut, along with winter wood. Corn to reap and potatoes to dig. If only there was someone to help you. No father, no kin, and your friends are busy with their own harvesting.

Rocks to gather, vegetables to pick and bottle.

You work like a plow horse, but you whistle. Soon there'll be a wife to help, to tend your nest, to weed the garden, to mend your trousers and stuff your mattress, to serve something warm when you come in each night.

Will she? Will her soft hands spin your wool, and bind your wheat into sheaves, and pluck the grubs off your potatoes? Will her china face turn bronze beside you as you labor in your fields?

XXVII.

No one calls me by my name. No one calls me anything, save Darrel, who calls me Worm. Mother never really tried to stop him. When she calls me, it's "You, shuck these," "You, card that sack," "You, grease this down," "You, watch the tallow pot."

"You. Keep still."

The warmth I remember in her eyes is gone, replaced with iron. Father is long since dead, and the daughter she remembers is dead to her. She buries the name with the memory.

No one calls me by my name.

Younger children do not know it.

I remind myself each day at sunrise, lest one day I forget.

Judith is my name.

XXVIII.

I hung the posies you left me upside down in the barn rafters to dry, to preserve them forever and gaze upon them always.

I was gone before they'd finished drying. When I returned home after my years away, they still hung there—brown and shriveled stalks no one took enough notice of to sweep away.

They are there still, so wrapped in spiderwebs that only I can tell they once were a young sweetheart's nosegay.

I take them down now, and outside, where I fling them high into the autumn sky, like a bride who tosses her bouquet.

XXIX.

I came across the schoolmaster near the forest's edge. I was picking pears. Two weeks new to Roswell Station from the academy up at Newkirk, he was out strolling in autumn dusk, and he came around a corner in the path. I pulled back and hid behind my tree, but he'd seen me, and he took off his hat. Longshanks, I named him. Slim as a hoe, with a face the color of new cheese and wayward dark hair that hangs before his eyes, so that he must always be pushing it back. So this was the teacher Darrel was rid of. Which of them was the luckier?

His eyes searched me as if I was a piece of Latin, ready for translation.

"Good evening."

He *spoke* to me.

I left, dropping the pears.

He pursued me. "Stop! Young lady! I beg your pardon!" He was quick for one so spindly, and he caught me by the wrist. His touch astonished me, sent me a warning. I felt myself shrinking, compressing, coiling ready to spring. Yet even so, his hand was living flesh. Would that he were you, out walking on a balmy night and wishing for a word with me.

"I do so plead your forgiveness," he said, staring down at me. His voice turned my stomach sour. He didn't relinquish my wrist, even though I tugged. His forehead was high, and moist. "My name is Rupert Gillis."

I yanked my hand away and fled.

I could have answered him, in my way, and put an end to all future attempts at conversation from Rupert Gillis.

Village folk will make him wiser soon enough.

XXX.

Roswell Station has seen its share of sorrow.

Sickness is a regular guest. Babies ail in the damp ocean air. Winters are cruel and last too long. Frost can destroy a whole year's crops.

We fought a battle against land-grabbing homelanders. Your father was our hero then.

Fire swept through one dry summer, claiming a third of the homes in town.

One year the arsenal blew up, taking with it most of our defenses.

Scandal reared her head upon your family.

And one summer, two young girls went missing within days of each other.

XXXI.

Unfaithful woman, he would say, plunging his knife into the cabin wall, drove him to it.

That's all he would say. The rest, I knew.

His wife and her lover crept away to Pinkerton or maybe Williamsborough. Perhaps they now live in lovers' bliss or shared contempt in a solitary cabin, miles west.

They left. And he, the bonny man, the militia colonel, prosperous farmer, deacon, could not satisfy his thirst. No Widow Michaelson for him, no, though she be blushing, skilled with bread, childless, and under thirty.

A pity.

For him it was years of gnawing.

Till he found himself a maiden.

XXXII.

To the village, his wife's inconstancy drove him to drink away his mind, until like a beast, he set fire to his home and let the inferno consume him.

To the village, he died a sad disgrace. Not a menace.

Not a recluse living miles north across the river.

Not the reason Lottie Pratt's naked body washed up in the river.

Not the reason Judith Finch came home after two years, out of her head, left for dead, half her tongue cut out.

XXXIII.

The widower Abijah Pratt, Lottie's father, lacks all his teeth, and half his wits. Lottie was all he had left after a bad crossing from the homeland. She was a docile girl who did his bidding. Now, as Preacher Frye would say, he's withered, root and branch.

He'll never meet my eye on the street or at Sunday meeting.

I came back, and Abijah Pratt despises me for living.

XXXIV.

The colonel was last seen alive the night his farmhouse burned like never a house should burn, with a bang and a roar and the walls turned to ashes before anyone could get there. All his things destroyed, he fled to where no one could find him.

You weren't there that night. It was spring, fishing season, and you and your puppy were out searching for night crawlers.

The whole village ran in their nightclothes to see the cause of the noise. Like Hell itself had wrenched a hole in the soil for wayward man to jump through.

You ran back with your bucket and dropped it when you saw where your house had been. The lanterns the townspeople carried shone on your wriggling, escaping worms.

XXXV.

My mother and father brought you home that night and gave you Darrel's bed.

You couldn't sleep. Nor could any of us.

Father fed the fire long into the night. You slumped in a chair before the hearth with my father's leather hand resting upon your shoulder, and Jip curled around your ankles.

And so you stayed with us for a season, until Father organized a crew of men to help you rebuild a small cabin where your old home had stood. He helped you plow and plant your spring wheat. He persuaded the aldermen to erect a tombstone for your father in the churchyard. You loved my father for all he did for you.

But still, I would find you sometimes that summer, sitting with your feet dangling in the stream, staring at the water with hollow eyes. I would sit beside you, and we would watch the stream together.

I was twelve then, and you, a skinny, under-grown sixteen.

XXXVI.

The evening I stumbled home, it was midsummer twilight, soft and blue over the split-log fence, the fields, the hills beyond. A sight I never thought I'd see again.

Darrel, still a boy, though bigger, saw me first and yelled. Mother burst out the door, wiping her hands on her dress, then hitched up her skirts and ran to me, calling my name.

We collided. She clasped me to her, rubbing her hands over every part of me.

Then she stopped and took my head in both hands.

Her mouth contorted with weeping. "You came back. Sweet Lord above. You came back."

I drank in her face, the damp summer smell of her.

"Where have you been, child?"

In spite of my plans my lips parted. I pressed them shut again.

"Speak to me."

"I ghanh."

Her weeping eyes froze. She grasped my face and tilted back my head. She pushed down my protesting jaw with her strong thumbs.

She cried out and released me. My head fell back for an instant, then I righted myself.

She stood with both hands clasped over her mouth, her eyes as round as the midsummer moon.

XXXVII.

I don't believe in miracles. The Blessed Virgin, he said, appeared to him and told him not to do this thing, nor take my life.

Mother would have called it a shameful papist remark.

And that was when he cut me.

XXXVIII.

Once, toward the end of the summer when you lived with us, I sat by the stream, plucking petals off a flower and dropping them one by one into the swirling water.

I'd flung the empty stem into the water and had nothing left to toss but grass when you appeared with a handful of posies.

"You looked like you were running out," you said.

I laughed and buried my nose in the bouquet. "You can join me, if you like," I said. "You brought enough flowers for both of us."

You smiled then. Green sunlight filtering through my willow boughs moved across your face. I realized it was the first I'd seen you smile since the night your house burned, leaving you alone in the world.

I watched the light on your face too long. Your cheeks grew red. You sat down and took a flower, plucked a petal, and dropped it in the stream.

When we'd stripped all the blossoms, we watched the water. You took my hand and held it. It occurred to me that I should feel startled, but it was only peaceful, there with you, with willow boughs brushing us like feathers, and the stream moving ever and ever past us toward the sea.

XXXIX.

I pick wild grapes, east of town. My knife slices through the woody stems and almost cuts my finger. Mother wants two bucketsful for wine. You're not Maria's yet, and so I make a plan to leave you some, in a bowl on your porch. No, I'll be daring and bring them inside, fill your pan with them. A farewell gift while I still may, and a mystery to make you wonder.

What do I care if it's shocking? I am shocking. What was done to me was shocking. I am outside the boundaries forever, no longer decent. I will leave grapes for you in your own home.

Galloping hoofbeats on the track shorten my plans. I duck in the bushes. Peeping through, I see Clyde Aldrus riding the horse that's kept pastured at the lookout. He's bent low in the saddle, urging the horse on with a face full of fear.

XL.

The church bell sounds its strident warning, a summons for all in the village to drop what they're doing and come. I arrive in town, panting, my pail banging my shin.

A huddle of villagers surrounds the pillory on the common. This is where we shame our sinners, but now Clyde Aldrus stands upon its platform, repeating his news.

There are ships on the horizon, twenty miles east.

So the scout tells Captain Rush.

Three ships that don't appear to be carrying calico.

XLI.

The men in town are silent now. The women buzz with talk of war. Goody Pruett passes our gate on her way to town and tells Mother what she's heard. This time she does not even extract her usual exchange of a cup of bark coffee.

The homelanders and their ships can travel almost all the way to us up the river, until they're forced to disembark at Roswell Landing. From there, it's not a long march to Roswell Station and our fruitful farms.

They'll take it all, for a price in our blood. We know they haven't forgotten their brothers from '37.

Ever since the arsenal was lost, all we have are private arms. Blunderbusses, flintlocks, fowling pieces, pistols. Ninety guns with which to face their hundreds. Ninety men with ball and powder, and blood for spilling. Ninety necks that will turn to face destruction, and hold it back for half an hour.

Roswell Station will not see nightfall tomorrow. Neither cloud-eyed widow, nor grizzled elder, nor fat-legged infant

will survive. They may spare the younger women. The whole
and healthy ones, at least.

You will not take Maria for your own.

Even I can find no joy in that.

Someone else will have her instead.

XLII.

Men look to Captain Rush, who sweats, and then they look
to you. Unspoken on their lips is the fear: who will lead us
with Colonel Whiting gone? He was our confidence, our
miracle. Remember '37, when he rousted the homelanders?

So they look to you, the son and heir, who never shot
more than autumn deer.

XLIII.

There is talk of fleeing to the woods. Of wagons and frantic
harvesting, women loading clothes and tools and only the
most needed dishes into wagons and carts, and vanishing
into the great expanse of forest west of here. But what about
the old, the infants and children, the wives soon to deliver?

Others talk of sending riders out, to Pinkerton and Chester
and Codwall's Landing and Fermot, to marshal a resistance.
How many fighters would return from other towns? Would
they not rather hold them here than face overseas invaders in
their own harvest fields?

Would they get here in time?

I drift from house to house, delivering eggs and bottles and
written messages, until my errands are done, and still I drift
and listen, for no one thinks to curb their tongues near me.

I drift back home and see the lust in Mother's eyes—if only I could tell her what I see and know and hear. But not even for that knowledge will she bend her iron rule that keeps my lips closed.

I find Darrel in the barn, sharpening the blade of Father's ancient bayonet. He doesn't call me Worm today. He doesn't say a word at all.

I find you at Maria's house, in council with her father and the elders of the village. Leon and Jud and all the able men are there.

I find Maria in the woods, huddled on a tree stump.

She sees me.

Her enchanting eyes are red and fat with crying.

I don't understand the desire I feel to do something for her. I pluck the reddest apple I can find off a nearby tree and place it upon her lap, in the cave of skirt that falls between her knees.

As I walk away I hear her pearly teeth bite into it.

XLIV.

Preacher Frye stands on the stoop of the village church, telling an audience of women to believe in God's deliverance. All sorts of miracles are possible. The river could freeze. A malady could overtake them all. Fiery darts from heaven could rain down upon the ships. We should pray.

The women, usually rapt at the sound of Preacher Frye's voice, slip away one by one, until only I stand to listen in the middle of the dusty street.

The preacher fills his lungs and then sees me. He empties them again, turns, and disappears inside.

XLV.

I pass your silent house. You're still in counc[il]
I'm carrying my pail of grapes, so I push you[r]
tiptoe inside. It's as neat as if you had a g[one]
So yellow, the beams you've split to build anew on a burnt
foundation. The scents of sweet pine and old smoke mingle.

My little surprise for you has been spoiled by this evil
news. Nevertheless, I reach for a pan hanging from a rafter
and scoop handfuls of grapes from my pail into it. My fingers
are purple with crushed grape skins.

Something rubs against my ankles. I smile to see Jip wagging his docked tail for my benefit, and bend to scratch
behind his ears.

Then I hear a footstep, and freeze.

You come around the post of your bedroom door and
see me.

You jump, and yelp, and drop the boots you carried.

A squeak of terror escapes my throat. I set your pan on
the shelf and turn to flee.

You're naked. Half naked. You wear only trousers, with
the brace straps dangling over your shoulders.

You catch me by the hand at your doorway.

"Wait," you say, then you start to laugh. You hand me my
abandoned pail. "Thanks for the grapes. I'll eat them before
I leave." Your laugh ends when you remember why you're
leaving, heading off to battle.

If I don't run now, you'll see my eyes fill with mortified
tears. Your bare body is inches away from my face. I haven't
seen your skin like this since you were a boy swimming in the
stream. Nor will I again.

Here you are, and you don't mind me here. As though Maria Johnson were never born, and I, never taken. As though there'll be no war tonight.

I can't stay, and I don't know how to leave.

You reach your arm high to pull your musket from its shelf, and with it, a wooden box. Letters are stamped in black paint on the side. I am leaving, leaving now, but the box makes me pause. I frown at the letters.

You notice me studying the box, and wonder at it.

It's far past time for me to leave, so at last, with all my strength, I do it.

XLVI.

P. O. Some other letters. *R.*

The box. The back of the box. I remember that box, and many more like it. Stacked in heaps, facing the wall of my cell, so I never saw the letters on them.

P, O, something, and I think the next letter was a *D.* I hadn't seen it clearly.

P, O, something, *D,* something, *R.*

He brought them in, early one morning, before I awoke, and stacked them around me like prison bars. "Don't touch these," he said. "And don't light any candles if you want to see tomorrow."

I obeyed him, even though tomorrow held nothing to interest me.

P, O, D, R.

Candles.

Powder.

XLVII.

The word has come. The men will march to Roswell Landing, four miles east, at river's edge. There they'll wait for fighters who've been summoned by the riders—boys with messages sewn inside their shirts. At Roswell Landing, they'll hold invaders back for as long as rocks and guns will last.

The smithy forge roars through the night as Horace Bron melts every scrap of metal he can find into musket balls. Women bring pans, and men bring nails and tools and horseshoes.

Women must gather the children in and march them through the night to Hunters Ferry, eight miles south and west, where it's hoped homelanders will not go—at least, not until spring breaks through winter snow.

Darrel will travel with the men, and Mother, she'll stay behind to tend to the wounded. My mother is a brave woman. It may be that homelanders will reach her before any wounded villagers do. She is neither young nor old, and she is strong. If she would smile, she would still be handsome. I fear for her.

I am forgotten, free to do as I please.

No one eats. No one sleeps. You bring Jip to our house and tie him to a tree. He whimpers half the night, until I go outside and let him curl up in my lap.

Morning comes. I milk the cow. Her bag is full and aching, swaying. She's been forgotten, too. War can do that.

I skim the cream, then find the last autumn blueberries in the woods and fill a bowl for Darrel. Sugar, too. Why save it now?

I run to find him. He's in town, waiting for the army, as they've taken to calling it.

I tap his shoulder. He jumps and spins, hands braced to fight. But it's me. He slumps, shaken. I offer him the bowl.

He looks at me. He covers his eyes with his hand. I see his lips are trembling.

Underneath new ginger whiskers, I see a soft face I once washed and kissed.

I want to say, don't go, little brother. Stay. Flee. You can play soldier another day.

He drinks the cream and berries, smacks his lips, and kisses mine. I thump his back, and take the bowl, and send him off to battle.

XLVIII.

You are there among the would-be soldiers, organizing them in ranks. Your gun is slung over your shoulders, your sacks of powder at your hip. You move the men and guns around—how do you know how to do this? Your jaw is set with confidence but I see the concern in your eyes. I memorize your shape, your stance, your walk, your nod, the way your eyebrows rise and fall to animate your speech.

You are our leader now, and Roswell Station worships you. Propriety abandoned, women touch you, wishing you Godspeed and blessings as you lead their men to war. Might I dare to touch you, too? My heart pounds inside my chest. Only a few short steps and a tug on your sleeve. No one could censure me for that today.

But you whistle on your fingers, and the ranks form into

rows. The women call good-byes, and you lead the men away. Women sob aloud, embrace each other, and turn back toward their homes. I run away, fleeing down the street, so my tears can fall in privacy.

XLIX.

Darrel once read to Mother the tale of a girl in France who heard angel voices telling her to save her people from the English. She dressed as a man and spoke with fire and eloquence. She raised an army and defeated the invaders, all for love of her motherland. For her courage and her passion, she was later burned to death, called a witch and heretic.

Do I love you less than she loved soil?

I have no words to save you.

L.

This day they'll come. This day you'll die.

This day we wait in agony.

Mother makes me gather wood all morning. Fires, fires for washing, steeping herbs for bleeding. Remedies. All the wood in all this forest will not stew from all its herbs the power to give a bleeding heart its beat back.

But we must be doing.

I forage for wood, glad to be moving. Rotting chunks of falling logs, damp with mold and thick with beetles. Won't burn well but it's all I find. Darrel has the hatchet.

The town is quiet. Quiet is all we have to hold on to.

Women gone, and children, and the aged who could travel. The rest wait at Horace Bron's smithy, a stronghold.

Eunice Robinson went into the woods with her sisters and her cousins. Maria stayed. She is brave, or reckless, too.

My wishes stretch across four miles to where you sit—up in a tree? behind a stone? within a bush?—and watch long hours slide by, slapping mosquitoes, waiting, desperate for riders, dreading sails around the bend.

LI.

Goody Pruett finds me gathering sticks near the track. Her dried-apple face is lined with years of weather. Her spine curves like a shepherd's staff. Not even the homelanders frighten her. Nothing frightens Goody Pruett. Not even my missing tongue.

"Why're you still here?" she asks. "Why hain't you gone on with those wagons? Goody Pruett's old, but you got your whole life ahead of you." She talks that way, always calling herself by name.

I tap my lips with the side of my finger.

"Foolishness," she says. "Run and catch up to a wagon."

I shake my head.

"Your mother's staying, too," she says as if I should be ashamed. "And your half-grown brother's gone off to the fighting. Your family ain't idiots but they've got no sense. And you can tell your mother Goody Pruett said so. Wait. No, you can't, or so they say. Well, good mornin' to ya."

LII.

Jip whines and claws at the bark on the tree. I try to appease him with milk, but he has no appetite. He watches for your return through mournful, cloudy eyes, peeping out through tufts of overhanging gray hair. Poor dog, he doesn't know you won't come back.

LIII.

How can I search for wood while you go to your doom? I find Father's rock and stand upon it. I breathe in, wanting to taste life as long as I can.

While you live, is there nothing I can do?

Deliverance. If not from God, then where?

Father, my father who lived and died—speak to me here, if you can, if you're able.

A swarm of images unbidden: Powder. Boxes. His knife. His face.

The arsenal. The town's lost arsenal.

An explosion that would leave no trace. A colonel in hiding who coveted power.

The mind for warfare, now armed with the means.

A stolen arsenal. And I lived for two years trapped in its bowels.

I sink down, trembling, to my knees.

LIV.

So there is a way.

If someone can find and purchase it. If someone's devotion and courage are sufficient to die for it.

LV.

This isn't courage. This is choosing a death that could help you.

You'll die, then I will. That's one end to suffering. If you survive, you'll marry, and how can I pass your house each day and see Maria there? Shall I overshadow your new life with my unwelcome presence? You must live, even if your marriage means my heart's death.

I could let the river take me as it eventually took Lottie, and you'd be dead before nightfall.

But if anyone could save you—save the town—I know who he is, and where. And I may have something he wants.

LVI.

In hours, all I know will be consumed.

All that have mocked me, ignored me, spat upon me since my return. They were once my neighbors and friends, even if I am no longer theirs.

Even they are worth a sacrifice.

LVII.

I must hurry before it's too late, before fear changes my mind. But when I pass by my willow tree I pause, climb into its lower branches, and remember.

Lottie knew to find me here, and I her. It was our safe hiding place, where we could whisper. I showed her a perfect robin's egg; she showed me a comb she'd stolen from her dead mother's things.

When she first disappeared, I knew she had run away. Both nights I waited for her here. I knew she'd come to me to tell me about her fella. I waited because I was worried about her, and because I never did figure out which boy in town was hers.

She was coming to meet me here the night it happened. I

watched from this tree, watched the man whose face I could not see. I've watched since in nightmares, sometimes taking Lottie's place.

When it was over, I climbed down to see if anything could be done. Coming down from this tree was the last free thing I did.

I climb down once more and retrace the steps I took that night.

LVIII.

I follow the stream to where it meets the river. I turn west, far upstream from where you wait.

I reach the rapids, where the river spreads wide and dashes itself upon rocks, rocks that I must step my way across.

I listen through the gorge but hear only rushing water, wind on dry leaves, and geese flying south. No roar of musket fire yet.

LIX.

I don't believe in miracles, but if the need is great, a girl might make her own miracle.

Even if that means enlisting the devil's help.

LX.

A miracle: your face, sun-warm, green eyes gold, drinking in the wind as it dances across your wheat. Your hands, encircling a new-foaled lamb, wiping away the caul.

A miracle that can never be: your face, your hands, pledged to me.

LXI.

Geese wing south, honking to each other as they leave the river valley to follow the sun. Invaders hold no threat for them, only the marksman's aim, and they are spared the need to fear it. Freedom is theirs until the moment life ends. No lingering in pain or loneliness or dread.

Squirrels scurry on crackling leaves and disappear into holes. Rabbits sniff the air and vanish. A fox darts across my path.

Then nature stills. The ground vibrates. Hoofbeats coming fast. I swing into the lower branches of a red maple, none too soon, for riders thunder by, swift and grim. Through thinning purple-brown leaves, I count: twenty-three, following the geese, heading south to Roswell Landing.

I close my eyes and see you. Your heart will lift to see these riders. Your spirits will flag when you count how few there are.

I would leave this errand, follow the horses, and fly to your side. If you'd let me, I'd kiss away your fear, and let you rest yourself upon me, and I, I would die beside you and count myself lucky.

Would you? Fear of death drives men to stranger things, unlikelier comforts.

Shall I die satisfied while you die yearning?

I slide down, scraping my wrists and face on rough bark, and press on.

LXII.

I think of the river bringing the enemy ships to you.

The river brought Lottie home, but Lottie didn't die in the river.

That much I know.

LXIII.

Closer now. I dread his face. I could not, would not picture it, over all this long-forgotten trail. Could be he's dead. Once that thought would have brought me peace, but now, God help me, I need him. Him!

Everything's changed, the trees thicker, the shrubs over-grown, yet I recognize the slim defile, the crevice in the rock that ought to lead to nowhere. It's the doorway to his little vale of tears, the reason he's been undiscovered all these years.

I duck my head and push through the gap. Now his face appears before me, set and hard with one intent. I blink away the image. Clench my fists. Take a rock from the dark cave floor in each hand. All my anger and all my need must not fail me now.

The taste of blood, the cry of pain, the last clear words that passed my lips, the sight of eyes yellow with drink, the suffocating size, weight, smell, the hands that clawed at my mouth and sliced away my voice.

The tunnel ends, and daylight blinds me.

I can still turn back, but I would only find ruin now.

LXIV.

The night I stumbled home, I entered a silent house. Mother wouldn't speak. Darrel hovered, like a frightened animal. A strong smell of liquor hung in the air, reminding me more of the colonel than of home. Father wasn't there.

I pointed to his chair. Darrel shook his head.

I waited.

"Died," Darrel said.

Not Father. I didn't think death could ever claim him.

All that time away I thought it was I who would die.

My father, dead. My mother, stunned. An emptiness in his chair, his bed. The eyes that watched me seemed to say, you had a hand in this.

"Died of grief," Darrel said, his face full of blame. "Wouldn't stop looking for you. Took sick."

How often had I prayed he'd look for me? But I knew he would look. I prayed he'd find me.

"They found your things by the river," Darrel said. "How come they were there but you weren't?"

"Hush," Mother hissed, and Darrel, surprised, obeyed.

Father would have welcomed me differently, and now I would never feel his embrace again. In truth, I never expected to see any of them again.

There was food on the table. No one offered it to me. I picked up a chunk of bread and bit into it. They watched me, horrified. I'd already forgotten how young Judith ate before, when I didn't have to chew like a cow to grind and wet my food to mush. I turned my face away.

Mother put blankets on my bed. She'd been using it to hold sacks of fleeces. She followed my gaze to the corner where bottles of cider and whiskey sat on shelves. Once a home brew, now her livelihood. She would not look at me, but turned back the sheets, then pulled the curtain that led to where she now slept alone.

There in my old trunk were my former clothes. They called to me from a sweeter time, when I had both a father and human dignity. That they were still here was a testament to hope. Mother hadn't gotten rid of all of me yet. My eyes were wet as I struggled into an old nightshirt, too tight for me now, lay on my bed, and watched the moon out the window.

LXV.

I rose in the night and stood silent as a ghost by the curtains that hid my parents' bed. Where the old faded fabric had gone sheer in spots, I saw a beam of moonlight find my mother. There she lay on her side, curled into a bow, staring at the wall, and stroking my father's pillow.

LXVI.

"Keep pounding, daughter, or you won't make firm butter," she used to tell me. "A goodwife's arms and back are strong!"

I knew hers were strong. Tight sinews tied her wrists to her elbows. When she rolled up her sleeves I watched the rare sight of her skin while her arms flew through their work. Her back stood straight and slim in dresses younger women might wish to wear, but there was nothing fragile about my mother. She was a hive of creation. She made things come alive.

Someday, I thought, I'd be just like her.

LXVII.

I wanted to tell her, I'm sorry, I'm sorry. Sorry I snuck out of bed to meet Lottie. Sorry I was gone so long and caused her pain. Sorry Father took sick searching for me. Sorry I'm like this now.

Ar-ee, sssshhar-ee. My gruesome sounds made Mother wince.

"Be still!" she'd say. "You sound idiotic."

She told no one of my return for days, bound even Darrel to secrecy. When at last the secret could no more be hidden, she led me to the shed and said, "You've come back maimed. I leave it to God to judge what brought this upon you. But the village will fear you. They'll call you cursed. Some men may try to take advantage of you. I know my duty to my own flesh and blood, and I will protect you. But you'll mind me and behave as a maiden should. Utter one sound to our shame, and you'll sleep here among the rakes and shovels."

Where were the hands that embraced me when I came in from across the fields? Where were the eyes that smiled at my little bread loaves and crooked stitches?

"Know me," she said, lifting my chin so I'd see her eyes. "Am I a woman of my word?"

I nodded, resisting the pressure of her finger on my chin.

"Well then," she said.

LXVIII.

He sent me back with these words:

"I spared you twice. Tell no one of me, or I'll send Roswell Station to meet its maker. Blow it straight up to God. Heaven's all they think of anyway."

LXIX.

Roswell Station was never as agog as the day the news was known: Judith Finch had come home, alive but mute. Mother tried to hide me in the house, but Goody Pruett sniffed me out. She only had to hobble by in the morning, and her sixth sense spotted something different. She needled her way in for bark coffee. Needing no pretense, she pulled back the curtains where Mother had hidden me in her own bed.

"Well, well, well," she said. "If it isn't little Judith, back after so long. And why would we keep such good news a secret?"

It was all over then. Nothing Mother could say would stop Goody Pruett from telling. I was glad of it. We might as well face the world.

A stream of curious visitors flowed by the house all day, till Mother sent me to bed and told the rest I was too weak.

You came that evening through your fields, alone except for Jip. I'd crept out of bed, dressed, and gone outside to sit.

Jip ran to me and laid his panting head in my lap. He got to me before you did.

You halted when you saw me watching you, and waved. You almost looked frightened. I waved back, and you came to me.

Two years had made you fully a man. I looked down at myself and remembered they had made me a woman, too, or nearly. I knew I should flee indoors, out of modesty or shame, but I couldn't escape. Two years I'd nursed thoughts of you, and now you were here before me, different and the same. We were four people: the children we'd been, and grown strangers now.

You couldn't look me in the eye. You watched Jip go bounding after a rabbit in the hedge.

I waited for you to speak. I wondered if you could hear the chaos inside my veins and bones that your arrival had awoken.

"Beautiful evening," you said after an eternity.

I looked around. It was, indeed, and in so many ways, to me. "Mm," I said.

You looked at me then.

My voice made you turn. Of course you would have heard my news. I lowered my eyes.

And then your words surprised me. "I knew you'd come back."

You did?

Then you knew more than I did.

"People said you were dead, but I . . ."

I looked up at you then. Our eyes met.

What did you say when others said I was dead, Lucas? What did you wish?

I heard your breathing. I saw your sadness. I thought of my dreams of you, and wondered, did you ever have dreams of me? Now I have come back, but not quite all of me.

"I . . ."

Still, it was kind of you to be sorry for what had happened to me.

". . . I'm glad you're back."

We watched two mourning doves chase each other.

LXX.

After I returned, the village elders summoned me to appear

before them. The village was barred because of my delicate
youth.

Mother sat behind me in the front church pew. The elders
sat on the platform, and I alone in a chair before them. They
placed a small desk before me and gave me some paper and
pen and ink. My stomach felt twisted with terror. Their staring
eyes reminded me of his, those eyes that never left me.

Remember how I spared you twice.

"Miss Finch," said Alderman Brown, "we must know.
Where have you been all this time?"

I twisted the quill pen awkwardly in my hand. My fingers
were unsure of how to grasp it. I could barely write. My edu-
cation was at Mother's knee, and she was no great reader.
Cooking, housewifery, and needlework were my training.
Later, Roswell Station hired a schoolmaster from the academy, but by that time, I was gone.

I dipped the quill in the inkwell and tapped it against the
rim.

I . . . dont . . . no, I wrote in large clumsy letters.

Alderman Brown's beard wagged. "Do you mean you
don't know the name of the place, or that you have no memory of where you were?"

No memory. The words were like a rope thrown to someone at the bottom of a well. This could account for everything.

I shook my head sadly.

They shuffled in their seats. Alderman Brown cleared his
throat. "Your tongue has been savagely taken from you," he
said. "Who is it who harmed you so grievously?"

This wasn't pity, was it? My tongue, taken from me. As if
it was a stolen purse.

I held up the paper I'd already used. A lie and a sin, but I did it.

"Did this person harm you in other ways?"

I sat like a stone, staring down at their boots.

"Miss Finch. It is vital that we know. You won't be blamed. Did he take your maidenhood?"

The church's dark beams loomed over, above me. The empty benches stretched behind, filled only with Mother, straining to know.

No, I shook my head. No. No. He didn't take my maidenhood.

LXXI.

I am close now, pressing on through branches and trees. My quest is almost over, though the hard part has not yet begun. I never dreamed I'd walk the road back to him of my own free choice.

And there. The hut. I clutch a tree.

It's there. Darker. Older. Smaller, or did memory make it large?

A thread of smoke winds upward. He's alive.

LXXII.

His knife sinks into the tree next to me. I drop down to the ground and crouch, covering my head.

I hear the door slam and his footsteps approach.

I feel him standing there, feel the shadow that's fallen over me.

I let my arms drop and look up slowly at him.

LXXIII.

"You," he says, surprised.

He uncocks the hammer of his gun. Retrieves his knife. He is dark against the blinding afternoon sun that shines behind him. I shade my face with my hand.

He steps forward, raising his knife arm, and I close my eyes. Behind my eyelids I see your face, white-eyed with fear, spattered with red.

I open my eyes and stand. He steps back. The hawk afraid of its mouse, the bear afraid of its trout.

He looks the same, but longer, stretched out. His steel-gray beard reaches his lowest rib, and the hair on his head hangs down to his hips. His flesh is more spare, but still gristly and strong, a man who hasn't surrendered much to the passing of time. In his murky, yellowed eyes I see desire, and anger, and shame.

He looks around. "Who'd you bring?"

I shake my head. A breeze blows through the woods, chilling my sweating frame. He looks around, suspicious, as if this breeze and noise are proof I brought some treachery.

"What do you want?" His voice rasps in his throat. He moves around, lifting branches, searching for signs of a posse.

Mother's rules can't reach this far, and anyway he knows why I sound like I do. I try to grunt your name, to form my lips in the shape of the word. "Woocush." The alien sound makes me cringe.

He scowls. "How's that?"

"Woocush!"

He understands. Only the monster who made me a monster understands me. He frowns.

"Lucas? What about him?"

I seize an imaginary gun and fire it. *Bam! Bam!* "*Woo-cush.*" The pitiful sound I make is nothing like your sweet name.

"What's going on with Lucas?"

"*Home-wlanh-uhz.*" I want to weep with shame at my helplessness. "*Sships. Waw.*"

He doesn't comprehend. I could shake him.

"*Waw!*" I shout. My throat is unused to this exertion, and it pains me.

Homelanders! Ships, war! Understand me! Your ancient enemy returns, the one you battled so many years ago. Doesn't that matter to you?

I blink away tears and squat down in the hard-pressed dirt. I think of writing but in my panic I can scarcely remember how. Perhaps "*I dont no*" are the only words I can still form.

With a stick I draw crude ships sailing up the river toward Roswell Station.

He watches me.

"Made you an artist, didn't I?" he says. This strikes him funny, and he snorts a little.

LXXIV.

I turn to leave. He grabs my wrist.

"Wait," he says. "How many ships?"

Wait?

Three, my fingers tell him. He nods, his eyes narrow, calculating.

"Homelanders." It isn't a question. I nod.

"So, they're coming back to wipe out Roswell Station. About time." His laugh rattles in his throat. "We sure sent 'em an invitation last time, didn't we?"

I make a sound of protest.

"What, you want to be the hero now?"

The hero.

"Woocush!"

He shrugs, then laughs. "You sweet on that young whelp? I'll bet he fancies you, handsome girl you turned out to be."

The cruelty stings. We both know my face is plainer than plain.

I stamp my boot on the scribble that is Roswell Station.

"Good riddance to it," he says. "They ain't worth saving. Why d'you care?"

I let my face show nothing. He leans closer, whispering, his foul breath hot in my face.

"Bet they treat you real good now."

I try to keep my face still, but he knows his dagger has hit its mark. He knew exactly how they'd treat me when he sent me home this way.

"Who among 'em ever did you right?" he says. "Name one."

LXXV.

"Sit a bit," the colonel says. "I'll brew you a cup."

I shake my head.

There is a rumble in the distance. Gunfire, not far off. Each crack could find your breast.

He sniffs the wind like a hungry bear and turns to find the source of the rumbling guns.

"Ahh." He hears a sound he's long waited for, the sound that points a warrior toward his own true north.

I tug at his arm and point to the noise.

He shakes his head. "That's got nothing to do with me. Lucas is a man now. He can look after hisself."

The eagerness in his eyes belies his words.

LXXVI.

What husk of a man cares nothing for his son?

He won't go. Not for you. Not for revenge, nor for the carnal love of the hunt.

I can't say I ever expected different.

I have come this far; will I go yet further? Do I have that kind of courage? Will I light the pyre that would burn my body at the stake like the French girl?

I've watched you open your door each morning, these two years since I came back. Watched your throat swallow cold creek water, heard your feet tread through the forest leaves, seen your hands steer your plow. Were all your labors and your living for nothing? All the beauty you brought into my life, shall it go unpaid?

I take hold of his jacket.

"You, go," I say, clear as a bell. *"Hepp Woocush. I shay heyah."*

He turns to face me. He strokes his beard, looking me up and down.

"If I go win Lucas's little war for him, you'll stay here?"

I can't swallow. I nod.

"In what sense?"

Must he ask me that?

This is a word I can say. I've whispered it to myself a thousand times, when I've thought of you.

I whisper it now.

"How's that again?" he demands, chucking my chin with his hand so I'll look at him. "In what sense will you stay?"

I look at his filthy clothes, his leathered skin, his wire muscles over iron bones.

"Wife," I say, as anyone might say it.

LXXVII.

His eyes awaken. He licks his lips. "Promise?"

When I don't respond, he drags a lazy fingertip over the knob of his knife handle. "Doesn't go well for folks that break a promise to Ezra Whiting."

I think of your mother, and wonder, with dread, whether she reached her lovers' paradise.

"Or for their families."

Mother.

What have I said?

I am soaked in fear.

It's too late to turn back. Yet it's too late for any other help, either. This is why I came.

I nod to him and point toward the river. "Go!"

He grins, then scurries into activity. Should I be flattered? He leads a mare around the corner of his hut, one he didn't have before. She's dapple-gray and beautiful. I don't remember hearing of a stolen horse in town. I stroke her nose, drawing comfort from her while I wait for him to harness her to a small cart. How could a horse have gotten through the crevice that leads here?

He disappears inside and returns with parcels and jars stuffed in sacks slung over his shoulder. He's lashed on a belt that holds a knife, a pot, a flint, and other devices I don't understand, his dark tools. He fills the cart with dark powder cases and guns. There's more powder inside. I remember it. But he brings plenty.

How quick his movements, almost clumsy with excitement. My whole body is dissolving, pouring into my stomach.

He climbs a stump to mount his horse, then turns to me. "You coming?"

LXXVIII.

Guns report across the miles.

He can save you, if he will. If you haven't died already.

This will be my burning, my sacred sacrifice. I never heard any angel voice but yours.

LXXIX.

I ride behind him, his unwashed body leaning into mine. I swallow down an urge to retch.

He guides the mare away from the only entrance to the valley that I know. He leads us through thick brush and trees toward a shale wall to the north. I hold my breath. I can see no way out. Perhaps a young man climbing could exit, but no beast. But the horse steps from shelf to shelf, pulling her rattling little cart on a barely visible path, until I close my eyes in terror. She's as nimble as a goat.

We're trotting. I open my eyes. We're out. Marvelous animal!

We are only half a mile from the river, but each moment

may mean we're too late. Still the sounds ring out, sounds I dreaded but now they give me hope. The ambush isn't over yet. Perhaps more riders came. With each shot I picture the battle, and now it's Darrel's face I see, and Mother's, bending low to tend the wounded. Not you, please God, whatever god there be.

LXXX.

Take me away from this wretched saddle and bargain.

Anyone, anything, take me away. The horse's gait, or my wayward mind, deliver me.

No. I'm glad to go to the battlefront. I have nothing to fear there except returning.

LXXXI.

I had another young friend, a playmate. Abigail Pawling, the tanner's daughter. A quiet girl, like me. We used to play at dollies. I sewed a dress and bonnet for her dolly once.

After I'd been back a spell I wished to see her. I thought she would forgive my wretched sounds and try to understand me, for friendship's sake.

I found her in her father's pasture, watching their sheep. We gawked at each other and at how two years had stretched and changed us both. She'd grown womanly and plump; her eyes wanted not to recognize me.

I spoke her name, as best I could. She shrank back in horror.

It's me, I tried to say. I've just been hurt, is all.

She ran, leaving her sheep to their own defenses.

I went home and waited for Mother's wrath. But Abigail

must not have dared to tell her parents that the cursed girl tried to talk.

Fever took her the next winter.

LXXXII.

"Here," he says. "This is good."

He reins in the mare, and elbows me. I slide off, and he follows. Sounds of battle blend with the roar of the river through the gorge.

"Tie her up," he says. "Fetch my sacks."

It rankles me to take his orders again, but now is not a time for protest. I act quickly. He grabs boxes and bags from the cart, squats, and sets to work, mixing stuffs in a wooden bowl, rubbing them together.

I wait to see if he needs me, but he seems to forget I'm there. His fingers unwrap parcels, pry open vials and capsules. Too slow, too slow, and still the battle sounds roar.

It must bode well. Somehow we still stand. Do you?

I edge away slowly, moving toward the sounds.

Here the river sits in the gorge below, flanked on either side by high rock faces. I am only a few yards from the ledge, and from the noise, it seems the fighters aren't far distant. It was well planned to meet the ships here, before the landing, here where Roswell men have the advantage of height and cover, where it's hard for homelanders to leave their ships and reach our men.

Trees are thin, bushes sparse. I crouch and creep forward, until at last I'm crawling on my hands and knees. I can hear men's voices, murmuring low to one another through the brush, but I haven't reached the lip of the ledge yet. I'm not sure if I dare to.

Through a veil of autumn grass I see a man sitting on his haunches, his feet pulled in tight to his legs. He is folded like a cricket. Long white fingers twitch like antennae over the barrel of his gun. It is the schoolmaster. He pushes his hair out of his eyes and ducks low to avoid the battle. He revolts me—to lurk like this, while you and Darrel stand in harm's way.

I crawl around behind him. Rupert Gillis never notices. He only has ears for battle sounds.

I proceed more cautiously now.

Footsteps. I flatten myself to the ground and try not to breathe.

They stop directly before me, and a gun barrel waves before my nose.

I look up to see you train your aim on me.

LXXXIII.

You're alive.

Your face is pale. Your eyes are terrified. You lower your gun.

"Judith?"

You use my name. Not "Miss Finch." I rise to my feet.

"What are you *doing* here?" Your eyes race back and forth, over me and back to the gorge. Are you more angry, or afraid?

"Please go home," you say. "This is no place for you. You'll be hurt, and I won't be able to . . ." Your attention snaps elsewhere, like a hunting dog sniffing the wind.

You look like someone trapped in a nightmare. I should pity you, but I'm so happy to see you alive.

"Please go home," you say again. "Please."

Do you suppose I'm here just to follow you? I wonder. I could almost laugh.

I shake my head. I won't go home. Yes, I should laugh— I'm a wife now, independent.

Every gunshot makes you turn toward the battle, toward the men who venture forward, shoot, then scurry back again.

"Lucas," comes a whispered shout. "We're nearly out of shot."

You turn toward the voice, but I prevent you. I seize your hand and tug you toward your father. You resist, but not too much. Surprise, I think, works for me. You come. We both duck low through the grasses. I don't relinquish your hand. Hard-calloused and hot, damp with sweat, furred with hair on the back. I'm giddy in this moment, which is wicked, with puffs of dark smoke rising into the blue sky, and balls shrieking through the air, but I hold your hand in mine.

You stagger back and yank my prize away. "What am I doing?" you say. "Judith, *I can't come with you!*"

It wounds me to grunt my bestial noises at you.

"Come!" I say, clearly enough.

You stop in your tracks and stare at me. Which of us is more amazed? If you think mine is a voice from the past, wait only a moment longer.

I seize your hand once more, and you let yourself be led.

And there. I part the grass and show you your father, squatting, feverishly fashioning death.

LXXXIV.

You don't recognize him at first. How could you? Then he sees you. Sees me touching you. Sees how tall and full you've grown.

"Lucas."

You stare at him, and then at me. Your eyes bore through me, first through my mouth, then my dress, my dark memories, and you begin to understand—or think you do. Horror curls back your lips. I stand naked before you both. I want to sink into these weeds and crawl away.

I hadn't thought this far.

I've killed you. Killed your pity for me. Killed your father again before you. I have no tongue to swallow the gall I taste so well. For here you stand, and there he crouches, and all around us cannon fire rains down, and the cries of the wounded climb like geese into the bright October blue.

LXXXV.

One cry I know. Darrel. He's hurt.

Mother and Father and I were so accustomed to Darrel's baby cries we almost stopped responding. Papa's little brat, Mother's darling, a chatterbox in ringlets. Such a shame the pretty face was given to the son. All this I consider as I tear away from your father and *his* pretty son, for once glad to be rid of the sight of you.

I follow Darrel's cry. Too lusty to be dying. Bless his fool mouth, he'll have a whole ship's crew on him in a moment if he doesn't stop that yowling.

I approach from behind and find him in a matted hollow of tamped-down weeds, Pa's pistol sprawled beside him.

Much too close to the edge of the gorge, his clothing singed and spotted. He's whole, intact, and for a moment I can't make out what's wrong, until I see strands of smoke rising from his boot.

I hook my arms beneath his shoulders and pull him far back from the battle, under the shelter of a willow tree. He is solid but I am strong.

"Thanks, mate," he says, whimpering.

I drop him and show myself. His shocked expression reminds me of yours, a moment ago.

"Worm!"

Ah. Nothing changes Darrel.

I kneel by his feet and worry the boot off. Half of it is clean gone, and the inner curve of his foot is drenched in red. I suck in my breath, trying not to frighten him. With his boot and stocking off, it looks like something has taken a bite out of his inner foot. The heel and toes are there, but the bone between the ankle and large toe is bare and weeping blood.

I've seen animals butchered. I've seen abscesses lanced and other gruesome sights. But never my baby brother's own pink flesh.

I raise his leg and wrap my apron tightly around the wound. He gasps in pain.

If Mother were here, she'd be in a state.

I try to imagine how this could have happened. How cannon fire from the riverbed, or even the soldiers who've scaled the wall, could have shot him in this way. It makes no sense.

He lies crying on his back, staring up into the sky.

Of course! Poor idiot. He shot himself.

I bite my lips. There's no laughing at his white bones. But oh, the foolish soldier boy.

Tears roll out his eye sockets and drip into his ears.

His foot bound fast and propped high on a rock, I move behind him and lift his head into my lap. He turns and buries his face against my knee. I try my best to murmur comforting sounds from within my throat. A hiss through my lips resembles the shushing sound I made when I rocked him as a baby.

With Darrel, nothing changes.

LXXXVI.

We sit, watching the battle from afar, like poor children watching a party at a rich man's house across a pond. It has nothing to do with us, so we feast upon the spectacle. The sun sets, and the glorious sky purples off over the ocean that brought these ships on her bosom. The prize land toward the west that the homelanders dream of subduing is saffron gold. Fireflies wink around us, just like the incendiaries that burn red and snuff out.

The night grows chill. We huddle together for warmth. Darrel quivers with pain that won't let him sleep. He squeezes my hand so tightly, my fingertips turn white. He doesn't speak.

Neither do I.

LXXXVII.

How can this battle have lasted so long? What has become of

you and of the colonel? Should I begin to hope? Against all odds, our puny few have lasted this long, apparently without my help. Could I not have gone to the colonel? Bitter, bitter thought.

Do I intend to keep my promise? Am I a wife indeed? Do I owe my old jailer anything?

It was your idea, Lucas, to engage them here by the gorge, I think. You wore the colonel's mantle well. If you survive this day, your place in the village will be made sure, all former taint from him erased.

You'll be farther from me than ever, if unreachable wasn't already far enough.

And I'll be in a hut in the woods. Unless I want another tragedy on my soul. I remember his threats.

All for nothing, then, and no one to mourn me. The village won't even count it a price paid. Nothing for nothing is fair barter, at least.

No laces, no feast for this bride.

LXXXVIII.

Only the faintest trace of twilight left in the sky. Darrel sleeps now. I no longer have to hide the pleasure I feel at the warmth of his body near mine. It's a cold world when no one will touch you.

My father used to hold me on his lap in the evenings. I loved the sweaty, woodsy smell of him. He never knew me as I am now. In my memory, he is ever warm, alert, interested in what I have to say. In my memory I can speak to him, sing him my little-girl songs.

LXXXIX

You run along the bank, waving your arms and shouting, "Fall back! Fall back!"

I jump. Darrel stirs. What can be happening? A retreat?

Men scurry out from their hiding places near the edge like quail before a hunter's step. I hadn't known there were so many so close by. They run, crouching low, and gather, some under my tree. Without meaning to, I cry out, startled by how many men were so close all along without my knowing.

By the light of a pair of lanterns, I can see that the men on the other side are doing the same.

I begin to understand. And I wonder, are we back far enough?

XC.

Stooping, peering in the dim light, some men take notice of me, and their eyebrows rise. The schoolmaster. Abijah Pratt. Mr. Johnson, Maria's father. They wonder at me, but not for long. I am not one of the women and children who should be preserved at all cost. I might as well be here. Other men, the strangers from Pinkerton, pause to inspect me. What they don't know about me shows in their wide, curious eyes.

I see you loping along the edge of the gorge, your face lit by something bulky and sparkling.

There is a sound like a pebble dropped down a well.

Another. And another. Little thuds as the things land wherever they do. On a floor?

On the ships.

Then:

The earth breaks open with such a loud clap, we fall back

and hit our heads on the ground, me and all the watchers crouching under the tree. Even lying on our backs we see it, a wall of flame that rises into the sky above the rim of the gully. We feel its heat blast our faces.

Another roar. Another cascade of fire.

"What's happened?" Darrel wakes up whimpering.

"Fire from heaven," says the voice of Preacher Frye. I turn. I hadn't expected to find him here.

Pathetic screams rise up from the crevice, and horrid smells. There are more explosions, lesser sounds. Their artillery catching fire. Oily black smoke pollutes the bright inferno.

Two booms. Not three.

Silhouetted against the pulsing flames, far off to one side, I see the colonel pace back and forth. Does he realize we can see him? He's troubled. Why only two explosions?

"That's Ezra Whiting," says an older voice behind me, sounding like he's seeing a ghost. Which, I suppose, he is. A ghost or an angel of fire.

"Ezra Whiting?"

"Can't be."

"Who's Ezra?"

"That's him, plain as day. Colonel Whiting. He's s'posed to be dead."

Your surname has started a fire of its own, here where we sit cowering before our deliverance.

"Ezra!" A man calls out.

"What brung him here?"

You freeze. You hear their voices. In the dark, you can't

see your watchers, so you forgot we could see both of you. "Where in Jesus's name has he been all this time?"

XCI.

Your army may be in a stupor, but you are not. With urgent cries, you summon your men to your side. You train your aim on something in the gorge below.

The third ship. Those men will be desperate now. Perhaps they are swarming off their decks and risking the perilous climb for a last, desperate battle. Even one ship full of home-landers is more than enough men. And they will fight like wounded bears.

I watch Roswell Station men load and shoot. Boys Darrel's age frantically help load guns. Whining bullets land in the dust, not far from where we sit. I tug Darrel backward as much as I can.

I see, in silhouette, a Roswell Station man collapse to the ground.

Was it not enough, the aid I brought?

XCII.

No one else is looking at your father. No one else but me sees Abijah Pratt walk straight toward him and slam him in the shoulders with both fists.

The colonel topples like mown hay. Now others see, and you do, too. You're on Abijah Pratt in seconds, yanking him off your father's body.

Abijah Pratt's arms windmill in the air, his screams rise over the shrieking fire. Someone helps your father up. He dusts himself off and stalks away, trying not to seem to favor one knee.

Abijah attacking the colonel! Now, while we fight for our lives? Does Abijah blame the colonel for his daughter's death? Will others do the same when they thread together his incriminating history? This man, thought dead, emerges from the woods loaded with gunpowder, and stands a likely culprit for all that's gone wrong since he left.

When they scuffled, it formed in me a vivid impression, but of what, I do not know. Like a familiar tune that takes you back to the last time that you heard it sung, with all the sensations of that moment, which make no sense in the present time.

XCIII.

A handful of men restrain Abijah Pratt. Your father's eyes are wild as he circles, taking them all in. Like a caged animal, coiling to strike.

Abijah Pratt makes another feint in the colonel's direction.

Still gunshots ring through the gorge. Your father looks past Abijah to the commotion there, like a man in a trance. He bends down and picks up the bundle he was tending. He works at it feverishly. The other men watch in silence, as if they have entered his trance.

A spark, and then another. The colonel holds the prize aloft and waves at the others to fall back. He sets his sights on something below and starts a limping canter toward it.

We both realize at the same moment. I know. Your "No!" could reach across the ocean to the homelanders' wives and children.

You break ranks to catch him.

No.

He leaps from the edge, for a second his legs spinning like Abijah's arms.

He drops from view.

Your back, your shoulders, your legs heave forward.

No.

Mr. Johnson tackles you. You fall upon him.

A roar shakes the earth. A flash of light like noonday.

Dark figures pull you both from the precipice and the quivering heat.

When all is sorted out, the last ship, too, is ashes, and your father with it.

XCIV.

The final explosion dwarfs the others.

The shouts and cries I heard from the riverbed will echo in my mind forever and make me wonder if my choice was good.

Is it comfort enough to know that they'd have done it to us if they could? And were it not for the miracle you've wrought today, they would. Good war-makers we are, you and I.

XCV.

They hold you pinioned like a prisoner, with your struggling arms behind you. They don't let go until they're sure you won't leap after him to save him. I bless the men protecting you.

In the column of fire, I see you turn and search among the dark watchers. You find me, and we gaze at each other.

You and I both know it. You and I both will feel it.

XCVI.

He is dead.

Swiftly dead. No suffering, no waiting, no remembering.

His tale will be told for generations. He's the hero in the flames.

A coward, more like, that he should snatch glory and immortality and die burning like a sun, rather than sink slowly into the grave confessing his sins.

I will never see his face again, except in nightmares. I am rid of my promise to him. He can never threaten nor frighten me again.

Then why do I cry at his dying?

XCVII.

Smoke eats a hole in the dark sky.

Darrel lies maimed before me.

Your father is dead.

The homelanders are extinct, their bodies flying up to the stars. I won't have to see this thing that I have done.

Survivors search with lighted branches for the injured and the dead.

The river churns and swirls over ink-black stones, singing its endless song.

And we are both alive this night,

you,

and I.

BOOK TWO

I.

The horse. The dappled mare. Where could she be after all this commotion? I haven't even the means to whistle for her.

I shake my brother. I stick two fingers in my mouth and make a charade of whistling.

"Huh?"

Oh, the torture of it.

I prod his shoulder. Bounce my head up and down. Blow through my lips, spread wide by my fingers. I buffoon myself when I try to be understood.

"Whistle?"

I nod.

"You want me to whistle?"

I nod so hard it gives me headache.

"Why?"

I could pull out my hair. Better, his. I jab him again. Do it, idiot. I can't carry you home.

He shrugs and jams his dirty fingers in his mouth. His whistle doubles my headache. It is one of his few talents, so loud it brings others over to check on us.

"She wanted me to whistle," he tells them, making a face like *he's* the one humoring an imbecile.

I hear a rustle behind me. I creep back to see, plying my way through willow branches like a swimmer.

I can't see her but I feel her there. The sweet dusty scent of her hide, the whoosh of her breath. It's a wonder she didn't flee at the explosions.

I don't know her name, neither could I use it if I did. She is more shadow and fancy than flesh and bone. I christen her Phantom.

Murmuring low, I approach her with my hands outstretched. She makes a warning sound, and I pause, pouring warmth and comfort into my sounds.

She takes the smallest of steps toward me.

Pretty lady, pretty Phantom, do you remember me?

Wet nostrils nuzzle my nose, my hair. I lift a hand and brush my fingers over her coarse hide, the warm disk of her cheek.

I unhitch her from the cart she pulls, little more than a box on wheels, and lead her with coaxing noises to where Darrel lies. In my mind, I ask her to carry my brother to a safe place. I thank her for coming to me.

She bows her head and taps a hoof on the ground.

We speak the same language.

II.

I get behind Darrel once more and hook my arms underneath his shoulders. I wish Mother didn't always give him first crack at dinner. I can barely lift him up to stand. He can't mount a horse, except to lean over Phantom's back with his arms and upper body. He does so, and I give his good foot a boost. After some struggle and protest, I get him on Phantom's back.

The men with torches mill about. Fourteen dead, I hear one man say. Sixteen, says another. Others join them, and they confer. Too many injured to hike home. Where to spend the night? What to do with the dead and wounded? Who should send word of their victory back to town?

I could take word, if Darrel was able to tell the message or if someone had paper on which to write it. Darrel's head bobs on his neck, and his hands burn with fever. By now I'm not sure how much of what happened tonight he understands. I lead Phantom away, and no one makes a move to stop us or ask us anything.

Phantom wants to lead me back to the colonel's cottage. I consider it. It would be closer, and we'd avoid the river. I am curious to see what is there. Quick to the spoils am I! Perhaps there is a cat or some other creature needing care.

It will have to wait. I coax Phantom homeward, back to Mother, who'll be torn in pieces with worry.

It takes us nearly an hour in the dark to reach the river's crossing place. Darrel moans and shivers with pain and need for sleep. The rapids at night are nothing but noise and slick invisible rocks where a horse or a girl could topple and break an ankle. I stop and nuzzle Phantom. I explain to her what I need her to do and why. I tell her I won't ask of her anything I won't do myself. Holding tight to her bridle, I step forward into the river.

I miss a rock and find myself soaked to the knees in ice water. Phantom leans slightly toward me and I rest myself on her. Together we plunge and slip and splash across until soft mud meets our feet, then hard earth. Once I nearly fall and she nips my clothing with her teeth.

Are you catching me, pretty girl? Do you already know you're mine?

III.

He is dead. Your father, my jailer, my torment, the town's savior. I asked for his help and led him to death. If he deserved little better it scarcely matters. He is dead.

I remember once he brought me a dress. Snagged it from some travelers passing through toward Pinkerton, so no one in Roswell Station would notice it missing.

"You're bustin' out of that one, even if you don't eat much," he said, tossing me the rumpled wool. I waited for him to leave so I could change, but he made no move to go. "What're you waiting on, then?" he said. "Put it on."

I began to slide it on over my soiled, worn blue dress, but he stood and seized my collar. He ripped my dress down the front and wrenched it off me bodily. I cried out and clutched the new black dress to my front, then hurried into it as fast as my shaking body would let me. It was warm and scratchy against my skin, too large and long by a good deal, for which I was grateful.

IV.

We follow the path that leads to the village. It is past midnight. I think of the wives and old ones who remained, too weak to flee. They must have heard the battle noises, though they can't have known what they signified. How amazed they'll all be to know we've prevailed, that most are coming home. How devastating, still, the deaths.

We draw closer, and I expect to see women bursting out of their doors hungry for news. I dread it. It is one moment where I won't regret that people pass me by.

But we see no one, passing around the outskirts of town

to home. Darrel clutches the reins like a corpse. He shows no alertness, but only sways in his saddle, slumped as he is over Phantom's neck.

V.

Mother's frightened face, underlit by a candle, peers out the window at the sound of hoofbeats. I know what she's thinking—bad news, if a rider delivers it. When she sees me her jaw drops, and she yanks the door open. She's upon Darrel, gasping at his maimed foot, speechless with concern. She doesn't even mention Phantom.

Together we topple him off the saddle and catch him before his bad foot touches ground. We are the oxen, and he is the yoke we drag into the house and lay down upon his bed.

Jip, sensing the lights and commotion, barks fit to wake the town, but he can't be satisfied, for I haven't brought you back to him.

Mother doesn't speak, but a river of sound flows from her mouth, little sobs and soothes and clucks as she peels off his trousers, washes, and tends him. Half-snatches of prayers and endearments. Those who can utter, must, it seems, and those who cannot, lead the horse to the barn, stoke fires, heat water, cut cloth into strips to dress wounds.

VI.

Finally Mother can endure the agony no longer. She breaks her own rule and asks me a question that demands I speak.

"What happened?"

I gaze at her. Whether I answer or not, she'll be angry with me.

"The homelanders?" she asks.

I shake my head: they are dead. But she doesn't understand.

"What do you mean?"

I draw a finger across my throat. Her eyes grow wide. She falls into a chair.

"Who?" she says. "Us, or them?"

I tap my breast for "us," and shake my head. Oh, how to say this?

"*Home-wlanh-uhz.*"

"Yes?"

"*Gawnh.*"

She frowns. "Gone?"

I nod. Here are some sounds I can make. "Boom!"

Then she does something I could not expect. She smiles broadly and drags me instantly back to five years ago, seven, ten, when she was a happier woman. There is laughter in her voice. "Boom?" she cries. "The homelanders? Boom?"

I nod, and she claps her hands over her cheeks, then shrieks with laughter and crying. She rises, hoists her skirts up over the tops of her boots, and does a little jig. "Boom," she laughs. "Boom."

As if I were two, using my first words. As if she had lost her wits.

Darrel moans then, and my somber mother returns where the giddy one had been. Her son's injury is a worrisome one, but still, when destruction seemed all but certain, even she can be happy that the enemy is gone, we live, and we didn't lose the war.

It pleases me to think, though she'll never know it, that I had a hand in her brief joy.

Her voice interrupts my thoughts. "Do the others in the village know yet about the battle?"

I shake my head no. Will she send me now with a message?

"I suppose I should send you to tell them," she says, eyeing me shrewdly. Then she shrugs. "They'll find out soon enough. You and Darrel and I will rest quietly here tomorrow and see what we shall see."

VII.

I am home tonight. I didn't think I would be. I am home cutting bandages.

The colonel brought me cloths when my bleeding began. I had to ask him or risk his rage.

After my first bleed was when the touching began.

I'd be crouched, washing dishes in a pail on the floor. I would stand, and he'd be there, leaning against me. Then he'd walk out the door and be gone for an hour.

I would wake from troubled sleep to find him standing over me, running his hand down my leg. When he saw my eyes blink, he'd go back to his chair.

VIII.

Morning isn't far off by the time we collapse into our own beds. Darrel is as clean and comfortable as we can make him, well dosed with whiskey.

That is when Mother lets herself weep.

"At least Darrel came back to me," she says to me. I am

startled by this intimacy. But not the irony. I've long been accustomed to that.

Her eyes are red and puffy as she looks at me, as though for the first time.

"Thank you."

IX.

Once I tried to escape, after a few weeks there. I had seen that he went out in the mornings for some time, walked far off into the woods to do whatever he did. I gathered my courage and crept out the door. I began, on tiptoe, to walk away, in the opposite direction of the one he had taken. Twenty paces out, I sped to a run. Fifty paces out, he tackled me. I never saw nor heard him approach. I landed on my back, his face over me, his hunting knife blade clenched between his teeth.

He dragged me back to the house by one hand, whistling over my sobs, and threw me in the cellar to spend two days without food or the privy.

X.

Had I forgotten all of this? Had I forgotten when I went charging off into the woods to trade myself for you? What trick of the mind obscured these memories, and what further trick brings them back now?

XI.

He is dead. Not asleep, nodding off in his chair, propped against his door, his knife holster in his lap. He is dead. Annihilated. There's no body to bury, no remains to find.

I imagine his long gray hairs catching fire and curling up,

orange, till they all are consumed, till the flames reach his head, his body, his hands.

I can't relish it. In the flames in my head, his body, his hands become yours.

XII.

Sunrise finds Darrel snoring and Mother frowning down at his foot. My body aches all over, but what of that? I didn't burn at the stake, didn't even fight a war. I only took a walk in the woods.

I'm alive! And that's something.

I'm eager to know what the morning brings to Roswell Station. I dress quickly and fly through everyone's chores. It's wonderful to see Phantom in the barn. There hasn't been a horse here since I was a little girl and Father was alive. Old Ben, long gone. I groom Phantom with his currycomb.

I squat down and scrub Jip's gray hide with my knuckles, until he flops on his back and begs me to scratch his belly. You're alive! Jip and I can celebrate.

When I return to the house, I find Goody Pruett there, lecturing Mother on leeches and dressings. The veteran's awake now and making a show of his moans for our widow neighbor. I try to slip outdoors but Goody's shiny black eyes catch me. Why do I always feel she knows where I've been and where I'm bound?

I leave Goody and Mother and head into town.

What right do we have to such a glorious morning? Shouldn't the sky be ashamed of itself for such a vivid blue backdrop to red and orange leaves and grasses glazed with early frost? When have wood smoke and hay smelled so sweet, and fresh-gathered eggs felt so warm in my hand? When has our lazy old cow's cream bubbled so thick?

The cow doesn't know what to think about sharing her barn with Phantom.

XIII.

A basket of eggs, a bushel of apples into the wheelbarrow, and I hurry into town. I need a reason. I pass your home but you're not there. Of course not. You'll have stayed to help the injured.

In town, all doors are open, women whispering, huddled talking. Caps askew, bedclothes on, infants wandering dirty. We're all upended, duties forgotten. Word hasn't reached home yet, it seems. People stop and gawk at me as if they would ask me for news before remembering I'm mute. And why should I have news? They don't know where I've been. They look at my barrow to say, it was crude of you to bring goods to market on this day of apocalypse.

Maria ventures from her door, all color drained from her face. Her clothing is dark and neat, like one already in mourning. She sees me and searches my face. Like Goody Pruett, Maria sees through me. She knows I know something. She takes a step toward me.

That we both love you makes me feel close to her. I want to clasp her hands and bring her joy: Lucas is well and coming home! The gift of your survival overshadows rivalry. As if I could be a rival to her!

Even as we face each other, fife music reaches us, and footsteps. The villagers freeze. Are these the conquerors, come to invade? Only I know, and the secret consumes me. Down at the end of the street the men appear, two by two, bearing the injured and dead between them. Those who can are calling out to loved ones, those that do not dangle in blankets. The women hitch their skirts and run, their voices rending the air at the sight of familiar faces. Maria lingers longest, then hurries after them. I leave my eggs and apples to whoever will have them and follow.

Women weep, and men, too, some embracing, others searching for wives who've ridden to shelter. The schoolmaster, the blacksmith, the preacher, all on foot, and you, far in the rear, walking sideways, helping Abijah Pratt carry Leon Cartwright.

Maria searches the crowd and finds you. My throat is tight. She runs to you.

You see her, and you stop. Your face is a flood about to break, and you look as though it takes all your presence of mind not to drop Leon Cartwright on the ground and sweep her up in your arms.

She paws past you and seizes Leon's face between her hands.

"Leon!"

I stop where I stand.

"Is he dead?"

I edge closer. In all the talking and crying, I'm invisible.

Mr. Cartwright hobbles over with his cane.

"No," you say. "He's not dead. It's his leg. He lost a lot of blood last night. But he's alive."

Maria dissolves into shuddering tears.

You and Abijah exchange a look and lower Leon to the ground. Maria rubs him up and down, his shoulders, his ribs, calling his name. His head bobs, and his sunken eyes open. His lips are cracked and peeling.

"Maria?"

She buries her face in his neck and sobs into his ear. He flops an arm around her.

Everyone averts their eyes but you. You stand looking down at your bride-to-be, at the net of dark curls that spills out from under her starched white cap.

Her father appears, his arm in a sling. He looks at you, then at his daughter, and his eyes grow wet. He pats your shoulder with his good arm and tries to steer you away, but you won't be moved. Not until Maria rises from her knees, snuffling, and looks around at the knees of the men who surround her. That's as far as she gets. It's safer to look back at Leon's face, which has some color now, and wipe her tears off his cheeks.

Only then do you retreat and disappear into the crowd.

XIV.

You send a rider to summon back the escapees to Hunters Ferry. You see the wounded to their homes, then organize return parties to bring back more dead. You tell new widows how their husbands fought and died valiantly. You tell them their sacrifices saved Roswell Station. Alderman Brown stands on the sidelines and watches.

I watch through the parlor window as you carry Leon in your two arms and place him on the couch in Maria's father's home. You shake her father's hand, and bow to Maria and her mother, and leave.

XV.

If you were mine I'd comfort you; if you were mine you'd need no comfort!

Brave heart, that carried her lover home unknowing, that sets your formidable energies now to gathering all the injured and burying all the dead. Sorrowing heart, to lose a father and a wife in one battle and still lead the village in its mournful duty.

I see the slice of your shovel blade into the hard, red earth; I hear the grunt as you heave the clay behind you and plunge the spade again. Hearts must wait while a grave is dug so Tobias Salt, the miller's son, can be laid to his earthly rest.

I would hate her for your sake, but how can I not love her now?

I would shout that Leon's a lesser man if I could, but thank God Maria does not know it.

XVI.

"Miss Finch," you say, seeing me in the street. We are back to formality. "Did you see Darrel safely home last night?"

I swallow and nod. Yes.

"All by yourself?"

Yes.

You clap your hand on my shoulder and squeeze it, like you would do to one of your men. For they are your men, now. Then you drop your hand in some embarrassment.

"He's lucky to have a sister like you," he says. "Lucky you were there to look out for him."

I watch your back as you walk away. You know that's not the reason I was there.

You know I brought your father to the battle and yet you say nothing about it. My fate, my reputation, are in your hands. I can trust your honor like no one else's.

If I thought I could never love you more, I didn't understand you well enough.

XVII.

The sun rises high. I can find no more excuse to linger. You've gone back to the gorge for more search and recovery. I heard someone say there were fears of stray homelanders who had left their ships before . . . The thought went unfinished. No one, it seems, has told the village all that happened last night.

But you are gone, and the skeletal families who are here in town are closeted together to cry or celebrate, so I let my feet carry me home to Mother and Darrel. Halfway there, I realize I've forgotten the wheelbarrow. I leave it. It will give me a reason to return.

Darrel is awake when I return. Mother sits beside him on his bed, spooning soup into his mouth. He wears the face he's perfected through the years whenever he was ill, the mask of tragic suffering, which melts Mother like pig fat.

But this time his injuries are real. Mother changes bandages on his red, swollen foot. The wound is ghastly, fractured bones poking out, and the angry red streaks on his skin look ready to burst.

"Did you see any sign of Melvin Brands?" Mother asks.

I stop to think. No, I didn't, not this morning in town, nor yesterday, either. He's Roswell Station's nearest thing to a physician, so we call him "Doctor." He'll want to drain Darrel's foot, I know, and bleed him, if he himself is not dead at the bottom of the river.

"Was he there yesterday, Darrel?" Mother asks. Darrel nods his head yes.

So many injured, what if our doctor is dead? He shouldn't have gone to battle.

"What about Horace Bron?"

Neither of us knew where the blacksmith was.

"I need to dose your brother," Mother says. "Sit a while and feed him while I get it ready."

So I feed my brother until the bowl is empty. He clasps my wrist with a sweaty hand. His lips mouth the words, "Not Horace Bron."

When the village has a need for one, Horace does the amputations.

XVIII.

I go outside to see Phantom. I bring her a handful of apples, then take her out for some exercise. We have a fenced pasture for our cow, so I let Phantom run there. She shows me what she thinks of our fence by vaulting it easily. Her prance, her delicate steps, and the way her mane ripples down her neck enthrall me. To have such grace of movement!

Phantom leaps back over the fence and slows to a walk, examining the grazing. I watch her for a while.

A scream rends the air. I run for the house. Mother is forcing Darrel's foot into a saltwater bath. For a whiskeyed invalid, he's putting up a strong fight.

"Help me," Mother growls through gritted teeth.

"Don't touch me, Worm," Darrel yells.

These two have made each other what they are, and it's tempting to pull up a chair and watch the battle from a safe distance. What to do? Do I have an allegiance? Mother knows her business when it comes to wounds. If Darrel's foot has any chance, it's in Mother's hands.

I couldn't talk sense into Darrel even if I had a tongue, so I sit behind him on the bed and wrestle his arms to his back so he'll stop thrashing at Mother. He's stronger than me, but I grind my chin into his back.

"That's the way," Mother says, approving.

Darrel retaliates by flopping back suddenly and smacking my skull against his headboard.

"Now you've gone and splashed me." Mother is indignant. My head hurts so badly, I can't even feel the pain.

I can save a village, I can surrender my heart's desire, but neither I nor Mother nor all the homelander fleet can make my brother do what he doesn't want to.

The battle for Darrel's foot has begun.

XIX.

The touching grew worse. I learned to prevent it, to some small degree, by making myself hunched and still and small. But it didn't matter. His eyes never left me, not even for sleep. He gave up drink so he could stare at me, day and night. There was never a time when I looked at him when I did not find him looking back. The fear that clenched my stomach never grew easier to bear for its familiarity.

One day he sprang from his chair as I walked past his bed. He pinned me there, pressing his stale mouth against my lips. His hands ripped at my dress, savaged my breasts, then hoisted the hem of my skirt up high.

Here it comes, I thought, with a numb calm that I cannot explain.

Then he stopped as if seized, and tore himself up with a roar. He burst out the door, bellowing.

I sat up and plucked at my ruined dress and planned in my head the stitches to mend it.

I heard a splash and a bubbling sound. The door was yanked open, and there he stood, dripping, greasy, streaming with rain-barrel water.

He spoke of the Blessed Virgin.

Then he pinned me once more, pried open my mouth, swept out his knife, and silenced me, crying, "No more, no more!"

XX.

You came and got Jip when I wasn't aware. I must have been indoors scrubbing the wash.

"We can't afford a horse," Mother announces at supper. Supper—three roasted potatoes. That's all we have the stomach for. And Darrel won't touch his. The skins are burnt, and they smell. So do the herbs Mother's been mucking with for Darrel's foot. It makes my headache throb.

"Where did you get a horse, anyway?"

When she does this, she always pauses as if waiting for an answer, then sniffs just a little, as if I'm to blame for my silence. A perpetual reminder of my flaw and its aggravation to her.

"I won't have someone coming after us for horse thieves.

Was it one of them fighters from Pinkerton?"

"No, Mother, it wasn't," Darrel says.

It takes all my strength to hide my surprise.

"The horse is Worm's now if she wants it."

How does he know? What did he see?

"Well, she doesn't want it," Mother says, "for we can't afford to keep it, and that's that."

Smoke and dusty herb scents are so close, they suffocate me.

Darrel thrashes in his bedsheets, grumbling. "Fine animal. Shame to part with it. Might be useful with my bad foot come winter."

She glowers at him. "And I suppose you'll be handling its keep?"

She doesn't look up to see me leave.

XXI.

It's full dark, but I have to get out of the house. I'd rather sleep in the straw beside Phantom than listen to Mother anymore tonight.

The sky is bright with stars, the air cold and clean. It calms me. I lean against our fence. Some of my ire floats away on the breeze.

The wheelbarrow. I never fetched it.

Are you back?

Some others, at least, must be. Could the wagons have returned already? The rescue work must be done.

I don't need to see my way to find my way. I should have taken a shawl but I won't go back in for it.

Your house is dark. Surely you're not in bed yet. Perhaps

I'll find you in town. This puts a spring in my steps.

I hurry into town. Lights are on in many windows, including Melvin Brands's. He's doctoring someone on his kitchen table. I can't see his patient's face, but I see a pale body and a mess of red. I hurry on.

My wheelbarrow, empty, leans against the wall on Abe Duddy's store porch. I wheel it away and make my way slowly back, watching and listening for signs of life. No wagons yet, it seems. Perhaps they'll return tomorrow.

No reason for hurry now. I wend my way home, listening to the axle squeak and the wheel crunch over twigs and leaves.

I round the bend in the road and see a light in your window. I leave the wheelbarrow where it stands, lest its sound betray me, and creep toward your house. Night covers me. I hide behind an oak not far from your window.

The candle gutters on the table's edge. Your fire is unlit. You sit at your table, your body slumped, your head down on its planks, your arms stretched out on either side.

I see no bottle.

Are your shoulders shaking?

Cold wind blows through me. Night birds call. I have stayed too long, past decency, even by my measure. But I cannot take my eyes off you.

And then I jump, for you raise your arms high in the air and bring them crashing down upon the table.

The candle falls. Its light is snuffed.

Your weeping reaches through the window and drives me away. You lost your love, and it broke your heart.

I slip away. For this, even I will give you privacy.

XXII.

Next morning I race the sun to bring back the wheelbarrow I left by your gate, lest you find it. I bring it home, load it full, and wheel it back into town. Today I cannot fail to collect payment or Mother will have a fit.

I still see no sign of you. Perhaps you'll take extra rest this morning. I hope so.

But when I return home an hour later, there you are, coming out of my house, tipping your hat to Mother. I pause in my steps. You were here and I was not?

I go inside, determined not to let my disappointment show.

"Lucas came to inquire after me, Worm," Darrel calls out from the bed, where his foot is propped on pillows.

I look to him for more.

"Wondered if we needed anything."

Your own hopes shattered, yet you visit Darrel. Who would want to visit Darrel? You are good. No one knows it like I do. Maria never did, bless her ebony curls, long may they twine around Leon Cartwright's fingers.

XXIII.

The sojourners return, and the next day the whole village gathers at the church for an evening service for the dead. The village takes on an almost festive air, though soil on our twenty graves lies all too fresh for that.

Mother won't go. Tending the injured is her fair excuse. Darrel's fever's back, and his foot smells putrid. I spend the day doing all that can be done, which isn't much, and finally drift off to town. I can sit in the back corner unnoticed. I want to know what's said.

Abijah Pratt turns to stare at me from under his heavy brows. He sucks perpetually on his lower lip.

I slide into my corner seat and hide in the shadows.

I snatch a few threads from the whispers that fill the room. "Ezra Whiting" comes from more than one direction.

The doors creak, and you come in. All the whispers stop, all eyes watch you make your way down the aisle. They aren't smiling for their war hero. On the other side of the last pew I hear rude laughter. It's Dougal Wills, Leon Cartwright's pustule-faced cousin. You're now an object of sport, having publicly lost your lady.

The doors open again, and you are forgotten: Preacher Frye walks in with a limp, new since the battle. He reaches the lectern and grasps it with long fingers. His long black coat swallows all the light in the chapel.

Eunice Robinson walks in with her mother and younger sister, blushing to be late. She sits in the pew opposite yours and gives her skirts a shake. Her friend has cast you off, so now she's trying her luck. When you glance over at her, her eyes are riveted to Preacher Frye's heavenly face testifying of redemption for the dead who die in Christ.

XXIV.

"It was a shock," Maria's father confides to William Salt, the miller, standing on the stoop of the church, "when Maria broke her betrothal. But after all that's happened, I say it's for the best." He strokes his beard. "Lucas looked to be a promising lad. He inherited his father's gifts. But he kept his father's secret. No telling what else he inherited from Ezra. And now the judgments of God have come down on Ezra, for stealing away our arms. And who knows what else?"

William Salt murmurs in agreement, but his face droops. Still weary with mourning his boy, he has no appetite for indulging Mr. Johnson in telling Maria's tale.

"All in all," Maria's father says, "my daughter's fancy saved us from an ill-considered choice, and I'm not too proud to admit it."

XXV.

I lie in bed and listen to Darrel moan.

They think you conspired with your father to win the war. They think you've known his whereabouts all this time.

And Abijah Pratt is sure he knows who killed his daughter, now. He's made sure others know it.

I feel stifled by guilt. I hear the screams of the burning homelanders. I see the colonel leap off the gorge. Now I see the harm I've done to you by stirring up mysteries better left alone.

But how could I have known it would go this way? And what should I have done differently? I had to save you, and the rest of the village, didn't I? Didn't that justify going to him? Was it wrong of me to raise the dead?

The preacher named no names but praised the heroes who held off the invading horde like the Israelites of old—one man to the heathen's fifty.

XXVI.

What will become of this? What will befall you now that your father's guilt is back upon your head? Not even the war hero is shielded from Roswell Station's scrutiny. Will they haul you before the elders as they once did me?

XXVII.

Harvest must be brought in without Darrel's help, and hay cut for winter, too. I toil in the fields, and Mother comes when she can. I don't mind the work, only the sun scorching down. I have groundhogs and quail for company, and the task drives brooding thoughts away. The job is immense, and I must work faster than my limbs allow.

For once, Darrel hankers to do his chores.

For once, Darrel envies me.

XXVIII.

I let Phantom out for a run in the pasture, and once again she leaps the fence easily. This time she keeps on running, straight for the river. I follow pointlessly, then hurry back and fill my apron pockets with apples.

She's crossed the river by the time I reach it, and I pick my way carefully over the rocks. When the river is well behind me I take the chance of calling out to her, "Ooo-ooh." She pauses to linger sometimes, then sees me and trots off once more.

She leads me on an exhausting chase.

She goes straight for the colonel's valley.

I find her at the entrance to the crevice, for all the world bragging she knew how to get back.

I offer her an apple, and she grabs it between her lips.

I weave my fingers through her mane, and she follows me easily back home.

XXIX.

It is a day for callers. First Preacher Frye comes by to lay his hand on Darrel's shoulder and admonish him to have faith sufficient to be healed. He speaks with Mother in low tones. Her mouth remains a straight line, like the deep grooves in her forehead. His charm with women bounces off her, which makes him try all the harder, until he gives it up for lost.

"Haven't seen you at Sunday meetings lately," he says, and reaches for his hat and coat.

Mother answers the charge with a hand swept toward Darrel. "My son's illness needs tending." He waits before nodding to grant his pardon.

At the door he pauses, a hand on the doorpost. "Jesus said, 'And if thy foot offend thee, cut it off: it is better for thee to enter halt into life, than having two feet to be cast into hell, into the fire that never shall be quenched.'"

Darrel turns over in his bed until his back faces the preacher.

"Thank you, Reverend." Mother closes the door.

XXX.

Soon after, the schoolmaster, Rupert Gillis, comes. I answer his knock, then shrink back into the shadows when I see who it is. He doffs his hat to me and calls me "Miss." Mother's eyes catch all of this, and there is a glint in them I do not like.

"How are you, Master Finch?" the schoolmaster says, standing by Darrel's bed.

"See for yourself," is Darrel's lordly reply. I almost wish Mother would intervene and reprimand him, but she makes no move. She is still hard at work shucking ears of corn.

Mr. Gillis wets his lips on the cup of water I offer him.

"When you're better, Master Finch," he ventures, "perhaps you'd consider returning to school." He speaks to Darrel but his eyes never leave my body. I slip into the pantry.

Mother makes a small noise in the depth of her throat.

"Some learning might take your mind off your troubles."

Darrel makes no sound.

"We've no one yet who can raise a candle to you in recitation," the schoolmaster coaxes. "A mind like yours needs training up. You might be a teacher yourself one day."

Husks and corn silk squeak as Mother rips them from the ears.

"Thank you for calling, Schoolmaster," she says. "It was thoughtful of you. But as you can see, my son hasn't strength for much company."

I come forth to show the schoolmaster the door. His fingers brush my arm in the doorway as I hand him his hat.

Mother's eyes miss nothing.

XXXI.

The edge of Darrel's wound turns black. Mother won't touch her food, nor will Darrel.

Goody Pruett prods and jabs at the black flesh with her fingernail, and Darrel barely notices.

Dr. Brands does not sleep for tending the wounded, and we, a mile from town, on the outskirts in more ways than one, have not yet made his list. Perhaps the fault is mine for bringing Darrel home myself, instead of letting him be dragged half dead the next morning for his share in the spoil of glory for the wounded. Then the village would be more mindful of him.

I do all I can for Mother and Darrel, and Phantom and Person, which is what I've christened the cow. She resented sharing her barn with a named horse, lacking a name herself. "Person" was the furthest thing from "Phantom" I could find, and the best fit for her, cud-chewing bag of bones that she is.

I harvest the pumpkins and roll them to the barn. I fill my barrow with squashes and carrots. I trim the late parsley and cut the cabbages. I chop them into soup to tempt the sickly and the sour, but no one will touch my creation. I rub and water Phantom and Person for the evening. Coming back to the house, I see the moon hanging fat and low and orange, only a night away from full. I tell myself the moon no longer need remind me of him.

I collapse into bed, needing a bath but too weary for one. For the first time in days, Mother speaks to me from where she sits staring at the ashes.

"Tomorrow morning," she says, "fetch us Horace Bron."

XXXII.

I wake and ready myself for my trip into town. Darrel lies gray-green on his mattress, his arms limp, his face and neck slicked with sweat.

I take a last look at his bandaged, fetid foot before I set off for Horace Bron, the blacksmith, who can chop a limb with his massive cleaver if the doctor can't, or if one can't afford to pay the doctor.

Must it come to this?

In town the church bells ring, and people in Sunday best march through the streets. I hang back against the corner of a house to see what it means.

The door opens and Maria bursts out, dressed in china blue, with dried white flowers crowning her cap.

"Judith!" She seizes me by both arms and drags me inside. I stumble after her, shocked.

She throws her arms around me and kisses both my cheeks. I feel the two damp spots.

"Come to my wedding, Judith," she says. Her eyes glow and her cheeks blush. "Come celebrate with me, for I marry my Leon in half an hour."

Oh, she is lovely, so beautiful in her joy, it hurts.

She wants *me* to come?

I press my hand against my heart and lift my eyebrows. Me? She understands.

"Yes, you," she says. "I have wished to speak with you, but Leon has needed me to nurse his poor leg."

I remember last night's nearly full moon: today was to be your wedding day.

Still I stare, not comprehending. She understands and embraces me again.

"I have long since decided there is more to you than meets the eye," she said. "Your tongue may be damaged, but your mind isn't. You miss nothing."

I am unaccustomed to anyone paying such attention to me, nor even taking time to think about me for more than a moment. I lower my head.

She squeezes my hand. "And even with how they treat you, you are kind."

At this I look up in bewilderment.

"Kind to me, when I never gave you a reason to be. Not even before."

I feel my face grow warm with confusion.

"I have been a selfish, spoiled thing all my life, Judith," she says. "But I wish to be otherwise. Today I'll have a new name. It's the start of a new life for me."

I can't help my gladness at the new name Maria will *not* take today.

"Be my friend, Judith. Come to me in my new home. Sit with me and we will talk."

I close my eyes.

"Yes, talk," she says. "We shall. We shall understand each other. I am determined to know you better."

I don't know what to do but watch her.

"I'm a byword now," she says, her dark eyes sparkling. "A scandal, breaking my engagement to His Highness. But I don't care. I have my Leon. And now that people know Colonel Whiting was alive all this time, with Lucas apparently concealing the fact, I daresay no one will blame me for long. Still, I shall have need of a good friend. A friend with some intelligence."

I nod my head, too stunned to think clearly. Has she praised me or accused me? Her eyes appear kind, but what can this mean?

"Will you come to my wedding, Judith?"

I shrink back and look down at my dingy work apron and clothes. I shake my head.

She looks disappointed, and it occurs to me that Maria

Johnson is unused to disappointment. But she is in a generous mood today.

"I understand. You will come and sit with me, all the same? Some day next week?"

It takes some remembering how to do it: I smile. I will.

She kisses me again, on my forehead. "Bless you. Wish me joy?"

I smile again.

She gathers her skirts in her hands. "I must go."

I hold the door for her and we return, blinking, into afternoon sun. She hurries toward the church and I head for the blacksmith's shop.

XXXIII.

The forge is cold and still today. Naturally, the wedding. So rarely do we get a chance to celebrate, everyone in town will go. Even if Maria is a scandal for the moment.

All but Mother, and Darrel, and me.

And, I imagine, you.

XXXIV.

Abijah Pratt rounds a corner as I am on the verge of leaving town. He startles me. There is no surprise in his scowling eyes. It is as if he had lain in wait for me.

"Strange thing, seeing a female at a battle," he says.

I take a step back, my heart pounding. There are other ways home—I try to clear my mind and think of one.

"Almost as strange as seeing a man supposed to be dead."

I search around. There is no one else on the street.

The main street of town stretches behind me, and farm-land out in front, yet I feel cornered, trapped by his accusing eyes. I take one step forward, and he tenses. Another, to my right, and he leans the same way.

What are you planning, old man? Neither old nor young, in truth.

"You're only alive because you've got no tongue," he says. "Otherwise you'd be punished for adultery, you know that? 'Every knee shall bow and every tongue confess.' Except you can't confess, can you? So you escape the punishment. For now."

His words are insects buzzing in the corner of my vision. I do not grasp them right away.

Silence is the method I've perfected, adaptable to almost any need. Silence and stillness. I wait. I lower my eyes to the ground.

After a minute or two, he walks back toward town, swing-ing wide of where I stand.

My body is still but my mind is ringing with his words as I make my way home.

Adultery? Punishment?

What is he planning?

XXXV.

I make my mother understand. Wedding bells, blacksmith will come tomorrow. She peppers me with questions and I nod yes and no. After two years, we have our ways, when we must communicate.

Mother uses her frustration to peel a dozen apples for a tart for Darrel. We'll have our own wedding feast here, or else it's a farewell party for his foot. Her thoughts are far away, and so I slip out unnoticed.

Phantom's glad to see me, glad to eat the apple peels. I loose her for a run through the pasture, watching her tail fly as I gnaw an apple of my own. Even I can taste its tartness, faintly. It is as if flavors are still there, though far away, like a memory. But the apple is a hard lump in my belly when I think of what the town is doing to you, and of Abijah Pratt, and what he may plan to do to me.

Phantom's coat is smoother now since I've been brushing her. Her mane glistens. I'll need to think of a way to pay Horace Bron to shoe her.

Wedding bells ring out again. The ceremony's over. Maria and Leon are one in the sight of God and man. I feed Phantom my apple core and follow my footsteps to your house.

You're not there. All day you are not there, until I begin to worry.

XXXVI.

At dusk, I start roving through the woods. I hear the thud of your ax before I see you. You're chopping green timber. Still at work on your addition.

This is the hour when tales of forest magics and evils begin to seem more than tales. Shadows grasp at you with ghostly fingers. This is no time for someone grieving to be alone in the woods.

Your work would go faster with a partner and a saw, but you chop as if in a frenzy, your shirt brown with sweat. Two other trees lie fallen nearby, their pale stumps jutting up from the fallen leaves like broken teeth. Beside one stump, I see an uncorked jug lying on its side, and Jip lying next to it, half asleep.

Ax pounding, chips flying. Men have died from such exertion, and I wish you would stop. Whose face do you see in that green pulp?

The tree yields with a crack as it topples. A cloud of orange leaves flies up where it lands, and the chill wind sweeps them over you.

You pant. You swab your forehead with your sleeve and lean against another tree. You press your face into its bark.

XXXVII.

You sink down on your haunches. I see the boy I once knew in your huddled limbs and face. Jip curls up beside you.

You're soaking wet, and the wind is cold.

You lay yourself down in a hollow of ground, still clutching the handle of your ax.

Your eyes close, and still I watch. I am alarmed for you—this is not like you. I know you are assaulted on every side, by jeering youth and gossiping women, by wedding bells and memories. But this, and the bottle, these aren't like you.

In time, you sleep.

You're ill and exhausted. You wouldn't know if a tree fell beside you. But you could catch your death out here.

Should I wake you and send you home, and mortify us both?

No. I have a better plan, one that will leave you guessing in the morning, but that thought pleases me.

I hurry to your house where I take the blankets from your

bed and bring them back to where you lie. I ease the blankets over you, tucking them in around your legs, your back, your chest. You stir and murmur but you don't wake. Slowly I twist the ax from your grip and lay it down behind you.

The wind bites, and you're damp.

Then a terrible, wonderful thought bursts upon me and leaves me breathless. Would I dare be so wicked? What might happen?

The sun is fully set, and we are closeted by shadows. I take off my cap and untie my braids. The wind brushes over my skin, lifts my hair, reaches through my dress to cool my burning inner parts.

I crawl under your blankets and lay me down beside you. The ground is cold and rough underneath my hip. I press my back into the bend of your body. The feel of you washes over me.

The earth tilts.

Your sleeping breath moves a section of my hair. I press in closer, fearing each breath of mine might wake you, each gallop of my heart might stir you.

I look up and see stars winking down on my transgression. But sin and the dread of it can't reach this far. Together we grow warmer under your blankets. Jip moves and drapes himself over our ankles.

The stars' cold stare reminds me: worse than a sinner, I'm a thief. I steal the touch you would not choose to give me.

You'll never know you've been robbed.

You need warmth.

Night in the woods makes all things possible.

XXXVIII.

Bliss and agony together. I steal my bliss from your agony.

Every forest sound makes me nervous.

The passage of time reminds me of Mother.

Every moment I tell myself I don't dare stay any longer. Just this minute more, and then this, and then I must, must go. I'll count to ten, and then I'll leave. But when ten comes, the leaving is unbearable, the cold that flows into the gap when I move even an inch away from you is more than flesh can take.

And anyway, I must keep you warm.

More sounds. Small nocturnal hunters making noisy midnight steps. Even you stir. I panic. Now I truly must flee.

You fling your arm over me. It lies heavy on my side, dense with strength yet soft with sleep. Your arm is enough to arrest me. I reach slowly forward and curl my hand in yours.

XXXIX.

Is it minutes later? Or hours? I can't say. You pull your arm back and roll over onto your other side, turning your back toward me. In your sleep you make little grunting noises as you search for a comfortable spot. Sweet sounds, like a baby's.

Here is my chance to escape. Mother will be livid by now. And Darrel needing us both tomorrow . . .

I leave for him. Not for you, nor Mother, and certainly not for me.

I can't walk home. I have to run, for if I slow down I'll turn around and run back to my place beside you. I slow down when I see our house and frantically brush off the specks of dirt and contamination that could make Mother wonder. But all my worry is for nothing, for this time she has gone to bed without me. No doubt her fear for Darrel overshadows everything else tonight.

XL.

In bed I lie awake and listen to Darrel whimper. I marvel at my daring, and I curse myself for not considering how much more bitter I have made my future, now that I've sampled a syrup I will never taste again.

But even through my drunkenness and my worry for Darrel come unwelcome images of Abijah Pratt halting me in the street.

Darrel's cries sound like a child's. Mother doesn't wake, so I go to his side.

We're saturated in this, Mother and I. Darrel is not a patient who inspires pity. Only aggravation. I can't blame her for not rising.

Tonight Darrel's tears are not for pain. He knows what tomorrow brings.

I blot his eyes with a cloth.

"I'm frightened, Judy," he says to me.

I wipe his face and hands.

"It'll hurt ferocious."

There is no denying it.

"I'm not brave."

No one accused you of bravery, Goose.

Darrel's face contorts. "It wasn't even them that got me," he says. "It was me. I made a mistake with the gun."

He thinks this is a revelation; I pretend to receive the knowledge. I push his tangled hair back out of his eyes.

"Oh, Judy," he cries, reaching for me. I gather him into my arms and press him to me.

He's skinny, wasted away with days in bed. He stinks foully.

My heart is swollen with love for my baby brother, and with that love comes fear. Don't die tomorrow; don't leave me here alone with Mother. What kind of world would it be without your rascal face?

He relaxes his grip and we slide apart and look away.

"I smell bad," he says. I nod, hard as I can. He grins. It feels good to laugh together, even if softly.

Our mirth passes quickly and I have an idea. I pull the tin washtub toward the fire as stealthily as I can. The kettle is hot in the coals, and the soup pot holds water for tomorrow's wash. I pour them both into the washtub and refill them from the bucket. I add some wood to the fire, then tiptoe out to refill the bucket.

When I return, Darrel sits up and removes his shirt. He's excited. A bath, in secret, without Mother's approval!

Despite our efforts, of course the noise makes her stir. She rises up in her white nightshirt and cap, frowns at us both, and goes back to sleep.

Now we are less careful. I help him take his drawers off. It's dark, and I look away for his privacy.

I help him into the tub. There are still only a few inches of water, but soon I have more to pour over his head. I hand him the dish of sticky soap and a cloth. He attacks his face, shoulders, arms, and body, and I give his back a scrub. While he soaks I change his bedding and drop the soiled linens in a heap. Even his puffy black foot we soak a bit. Why not? It doesn't hurt him anymore.

"Let's send it clean to hell," he says, and I agree.

While he dries and dresses, I scrub his dirty bedding in the warm water and go outside to hang it on the line, shivering in the November cold. I look through the darkness toward where you were. Are you still asleep?

I go back in. Already the house feels lighter, and we can breathe more clearly. I help Darrel back into bed, smelling of wet hair and soap, his skin squeaky and red.

"Thank you, Worm," he says, and gives my hand a squeeze.

XLI.

I wake before sunrise and lie in bed wondering how much of the night before was only the substance of dreams. Then I remember what day it is, and I rise and dress quickly, my stomach a stone.

Darrel lies so still in bed, I fear we may be too late. I run all the way to town and reach the blacksmith shop before the fires are lit. I find Horace talking with some other men, Melvin Brands and Alderman Brown. I step back and wait in the doorway.

Alderman Brown, with his long gray beard, is venerable enough to risk talking to me.

"Fares your brother well, Miss Finch?" he says, coming out onto the porch with the others trailing after.

I shake my head. No.

"Is that why you have come?"

Yes.

"Horace," he says, not turning his face away from me, "Miss Finch has come to seek your help with her brother's foot."

"I'll go," says Melvin Brands, the doctor.

I make a gesture toward my empty pocket and shake my head sadly.

He waves my protest away.

"I'll go," he says, "and Horace will come with me."

XLII.

We march in silence out of town, pausing only for the doctor to fetch his bag. Horace's mighty cleaver is slung over his shoulder and he whistles as he walks. I believe he thinks it will cheer me.

I don't need cheering. I just want this to be over.

We pass by your house and see you coming out of the woods, your blankets over one arm. You have bits of leaves and twigs stuck in your hair and clothes, and your ax lying over your shoulder. Seeing us three, you halt, embarrassed.

The stone in my stomach becomes a jackrabbit. Thank heaven, the men's eyes are on you, not me, for I fear I'm turning scarlet.

"Morning, Lucas," Horace calls. "Gone camping?"

Bless Horace Bron. There's too much earth and iron in him to be swayed by idle gossip. But Dr. Brands, I see, doesn't greet you.

I look back to see how you take his coldness, but you haven't seemed to notice. Your eyes insist that I look back at you. You indicate your blankets with a small gesture, and wordlessly demand to know: Did you do this?

My face can be as mute as my voice. But it is hard to hide anything from you. I look away and hurry on.

I feel your eyes burning the back of my head until the path bends out of sight.

XLIII.

Mother has Darrel whiskeyed up and the fire roaring. Every pot we own sits full of simmering water in its coals.

"Excellent," Dr. Brands says, surveying the chopping block and bucket she's hauled indoors and placed at the foot of Darrel's bed.

A ruthless competence, my mother has.

There's a knock, and then you appear. For once, Jip isn't with you.

Must I forevermore turn hot and red the moment that I see you? Sin brings its own punishments, it seems. No matter. It was worth it.

You're combed and dressed and wide awake.

"Looked like you might need help," you say to Horace and Dr. Brands.

"Good of you," the blacksmith says. Still the doctor doesn't answer. Your eyes are like a child's, one eager to prove he can be helpful to win a parent's favor.

You look about the room, and when your eyes rest on me, they stare for a moment, bewildered. I'm seized by an unbearable urge to laugh. How disloyal to my brother, to laugh this morning!

Dr. Brands looks away from you and opens his bag. It is all the notice he'll grant you, and apparently all you require.

Darrel, praise Mother, is far gone from this world. The

doctor fusses with his bag of tools, with much examining and sharpening of cruel, curved blades. Horace thrusts his cleaver into the flames and turns it slowly like it's a roasting pheasant. You take off your leather belt and offer it to Melvin, who cinches it tightly, impossibly tightly, around Darrel's thigh at the groin, then forces a block of wood over Darrel's tongue and makes him champ his teeth down upon it.

At last, when all is ready, Dr. Brands looks at Mother and me.

"You women had best wait outside, preferably far from the house where you can't hear."

"I can bear it," Mother says, holding herself erect. She is regal and still has a young woman's figure. "I need to be here for my son."

She's magnificent. Melvin Brands looks away. I gather it's the thought of Mrs. Brands that turns the doctor's head.

"I'm here as a volunteer, Mrs. Finch," he tells the wall. "I will not charge you for my time. Therefore I insist you honor my conditions. The last thing any of us needs is for you to faint or become hysterical."

Mother draws in her breath, but our poverty weighs heavier than her pride. She turns and marches outside, and I am quick to follow.

XLIV.

It's a gray day, the clouds thick and low. Wind chases the last dead leaves around the pasture.

Mother heads first for the garden. There are only withered stalks now, and the root vegetables for spring. She strips seeds off of cabbage and carrot plants that have grown tall and woody. The seeds she puts in her pocket, then she starts pulling up dead plants and throwing them down, hoeing them into the soil with leaves. I join her.

A cry from Darrel stops us both. Mother grips the hoe handle with white knuckles.

We both retreat to the edge of our land, where forest and field share a troubled border. Without a word, we gather sticks for tinder, filling our aprons.

Darrel's cry is a constant whine, but far enough away that only a sliver of the sound reaches us over the wind. We can almost pretend he's a babe again, whimpering for a slice of bread. So easy to ignore.

I concentrate on sticks, on gray-brown grasses, stiff and brittle, quick to snap. Little knobbly pine twigs, their fingers barely more than needles, the best for starting fires.

Our aprons filled, we look at each other, Mother and I. We wait to see who will go to the woodpile first. Neither one of us wants to venture near the house just yet. If she's to be banished, her exile she'll keep.

Then we hear the thunk of a blade buried deep into wood, and a garbled scream, worse than any he's uttered this side of the womb.

Mother's kindling tumbles down and she runs for the house, trailing apron strings.

The screaming doesn't stop.

I follow after, but I keep my load of wood.

You meet my mother at the door and try to prevent her coming in. Your face is pink with heat, and there are blood-stains on your shirt.

She pushes at you, but you're a wall. She pummels you, but you don't flinch.

Anger rises in my belly.

Anger at you.

Darrel's screams collapse into piteous sobs.

This feeling doesn't know where to go. Who are you to bar her entry into her own house to comfort her own son? I reach the house and fling down my heap of twigs.

"It's horrible, Mrs. Finch."

There's no need to raise your voice to her.

"Brands is working to close the wound. There's nothing for it but for Darrel to endure it. It just has to be done."

Mother's weeping now, so loudly it frightens me. I've never heard this. I can't even understand her words. Your face is red with pity.

"I should be inside helping to restrain him," you say. "You must wait outside until we're done. Then he'll need you."

I reach my mother's side and put a protective arm around her. She twists and buries her face in my neck. I feel the wetness of her tears slide down my breast. I am made timid by my own mother's embrace. I don't want to move, lest I draw her attention to what she is doing.

Your eyes meet mine. They're full of relief. You think I came to help you. You reach out and grip my arm, squeeze your thanks. Before your fingers have withdrawn, you realize what you've done again: you've touched me. You squeeze once more—your apology—then your eyes widen with embarrassment. You flee indoors, preferring to face a footless patient than a pair of distraught, accusing women.

XLV.

I am sitting by the stream, some hours later, when Mother comes and stands beside me.

"He's resting," she says. I rise up and look at her. I would embrace her if I thought I could.

Her face looks swollen and tired. "It was his only hope," she says. She watches the stream where bits of bracken glide and collide. "The purulence was killing him."

I remember the thick, foul discharge she would lance from his heel. What I can't remember is the last time Mother spoke to me this way.

"If it hasn't already."

I reach for her hand and hold it tight. So familiar, Mother's hand, but I haven't felt it in years. She shows no sign of revulsion.

The paler spot behind the clouds passes its highest point and begins to fall. My stomach groans for its dinner.

A fat raindrop splashes on her cheek, and we both look up. I feel another on my face. Mother holds out both her hands.

The clouds that were brooding all morning erupt, dropping a curtain of rain. The stream drinks it eagerly.

"It will be what it is," Mother says.

She looks at me, then looks away.

XLVI.

Brands cauterized the stump.

Horace Bron, his face dripping with sweat, accepted our offering of eggs and bread and an apple tart in return for the wielding of his blade. Small payment, even if Mother's baking is legend. Melvin Brands took bread, and the foot, wrapped in camphored cloth.

He said he would bury it. There was no need for us to know where.

I wonder if he really will. I once heard it whispered, years ago, that he secretly studied the bodies of the dead to see how they were put together.

Now he can examine a foot of the living.

You took nothing, but later on you brought a fresh-killed hen.

XLVII.

I spend the afternoon capturing rain in buckets. There will be no end to washing for some time to come. Mother orders me about, but it's different now, and I'm happy to do her bidding. We have gotten through the worst, and now there's work to do, which we tackle gladly.

XLVIII.

If Darrel thought he knew pain before, he was wrong.

XLIX.

Days pass in weariness and dark November rain. Will the smell of blood and whiskey ever fade? It's too cold and damp to open windows, but at midday we do it anyway.

Darrel flinches and cries out. The pain in his foot is worse than ever, he says. In vain does Mother tell him it couldn't be; it's gone.

I think of Melvin Brands and wonder if Darrel feels his foot's second surgery.

L.

Mother rises hours before the sun to do extra baking for Abe Duddy to sell in his shop. Without Darrel's help the harvest was poor, and she fears for us this winter, even with her whiskey earnings. I squeeze poor Person's udders dry, extracting every drop of cream for cheese.

The hay bin is more full than last year, but not full enough for a cow and a horse.

LI.

You and Jip stop by one day with a cane you've carved for Darrel. Darrel is pleased and flattered, which makes up for Mother's indifference.

Jip's whole body wags to see me, and when Mother isn't watching, I break off a corner of a brick of cheese and slip it to him. He licks my hand lovingly with his long, pink tongue.

I'm jealous of a dog.

He has a warm tongue, and he lives with you.

LII.

Darrel sits in a chair at the table, and in between spasms of pain, he does small tasks for Mother. When she can't conjure up any more, she makes him read the Bible to her while she works. I envy him his velvet voice, his fluidity with reading.

He's still in awful pain but, he says, each day it gets better. The wound heals clear, which Mother calls a mercy. She changes his dressings morning and night, and every time he protests less. I have to force myself not to stare at the bizarre, unnatural remnant of his leg. Heaven knows I should have more compassion for someone who has lost a part of himself.

LIII.

I bring indoors a basket of eggs—twenty-one today, and at this time of year!—and lay a hand on Mother's shoulder. She shrugs me off.

So we are back to the place we were before.

LIV.

The trees are bare. The world is gray. I must go farther in search of wood.

The forest makes me remember you. By now, the shock of what I did has worn away, leaving only the hollow fact that I'll never touch you that way again.

But these thoughts are too heavy to bear, so I busy myself with the work of survival. I haul wood for fires, while you chop trees and haul timber. You're still building the room you began for Maria.

I haven't the time I once did to shadow you. The recollection of it almost embarrasses me. I've scarcely even the time to think of you as before, which grieves and puzzles me.

Then you appear, through the trees, guiding your mule as he pulls a tree limb. Like a soldier back from battle you fill my vision. You're a flood, a baptism I'd forgotten, and the force of you leaves me breathless.

LV.

I venture early and alone to church to sit unseen in my usual corner. On the way, Jip waddles out to see me, and I slip him a crust I saved from breakfast. We understand each other, Jip and I.

The new Mr. and Mrs. Cartwright come into church, pink and silly with love, not heeding the boiling looks the older women pour over Maria. She turns and notices me and walks over, thrusting out both hands to clasp mine. I take her hands reluctantly, not wishing to tarnish her esteem in the village any further. But she wills it; they sit beside me. This is their first time in the chapel since they were wed; they have no regular spot for worship as man and wife. Neither her mother nor Leon's family is happy with her choice.

"Let's both be lepers," Maria whispers.

It takes me a moment to realize—she's called me a leper! And she's laughing beneath her bonnet. She's teasing me and means no malice. I'm not accustomed to this, nor to such daring.

You take your seat just as the organ swells. Your eyes are hollow; you are elsewhere.

Preacher Frye reminds us of Christ's golden rule, that we should love our neighbors as ourselves.

LVI.

After meeting you head straight for home. No conversation for you today.

"Don't forget your promise," Maria says, outside on the stoop. "Come sit with me this week."

I nod. How will the village belle and village mute forge a friendship?

Eunice and her sisters watch us from across the way, but do not come over.

Abijah Pratt glares at me from the churchyard. One hand holds his cane, and the other rests on Lottie's gravestone.

LVII.

Darrel startles us at breakfast by announcing he'll return to school as soon as he's able. Could be there's a living to be had for him in learning. And studies are better than staring at the ceiling as a means of whiling away the hours.

Mother is unprepared for this.

"And how d'you suppose you'll get to school and back?"

"Worm can help me. On her horse."

"Worm's got other things to do."

Now you, too, call me that, Mother?

She's not done. "And that horse can't stay."

Darrel wisely says no more, and after a spell, I help him back into his bed for a rest.

LVIII.

I slip into town in the afternoon and find Maria taking up housekeeping in a cottage where Marshall Dabney, a bachelor, had lived before the battle. Now he sleeps in the churchyard.

I force myself to knock. I want to break and run for home instead. How does one visit with nothing to say?

"Judith!" she says, embracing me. "You've come. I'm so glad."

Marshall Dabney had kept his cottage neat, and Maria has already decorated it with a vase of goldenrod, and linens and glass from her trousseau, easily the finest trousseau in town.

"Come sit. Have some bread and butter."

"Are you well?"

"Is your brother healing?"

"Leon's visiting with his father this morning, so it's just us two."

"I received some tea as a wedding gift. Would you like a cup?"

"How about preserves on your bread?"

She has a pretty way of asking questions that don't expose my lack of speech, and it occurs to me, as she fetches the preserves from her cupboard, that she rehearsed this in her mind before I came. She wanted to spare me awkwardness. Mother and I can communicate, but not in a way that doesn't humiliate me.

Maria sits back down and leans her elbows on the table, then smiles at me.

"You are a lady of many surprises," she says. "I'll never forget that day you threw an egg at Leon. Lord, how it made me laugh."

I blush.

"You don't know how many times I've wished I had an egg to chuck at him myself. I only said yes to Lucas because Leon hadn't gathered up the gumption to ask for me first himself."

"Oh?" I say, then catch myself. Maria looks startled, then pleased. Her easy way of talking makes me forget that I don't answer. She has brought me back to when people used to talk to me, and I would answer them.

I reach into my little bag and pull out some needlework. I

am sewing a sack for Darrel to carry his schoolbooks in, one that slings from one shoulder across his body to the other hip. It seems like a better way for him to balance.

Maria continues her tale. "Was it wicked of me to encourage Lucas, Judith? Half the time I thought I would go ahead and marry him, just to spite Leon. I was so vexed at him, and I thought I didn't care. Then as time went on, I wished he'd be a man and do something. Even fight Lucas for me! Can you believe the foolishness?" She paused and gazed out the window. "And then when he was injured I didn't care anymore."

I can only watch her. I suppose my dumb wonderment shows. I am not sure what mystifies me more: that she should confide in me or that she should place Leon over you. But I am glad, glad, glad of it.

Maria's eyes sparkle. "Judith, I *am* just as wicked as they say. Now you see it's true."

Wicked indeed. I laugh a little. If she could have seen me a few nights ago in the woods . . .

"And what I see is that you are a person who misses nothing. You're not what people make you out to be, a half-wit. Oh, come! We both know it. You were as sharp as any girl before, though you never were a prattler like some girls, were you?"

Maria notices me sewing and pulls out some knitting of her own. Socks, it seems, probably for her husband.

"Isn't this nice?" she says. "What fine, close stitching you have, Judith. You could teach me, I'm sure. Is that a hunting bag?"

She watches me closely. I shake my head. Maria is not

content with that dismissal. I wonder if I dare try an answer. My lips practice the motion before I trust them to make a sound. But these are sounds I think I can make.

"Book," I say. My voice is squeaky, and somewhat nasal, but the word is clear enough.

Maria beams. "A book bag!" I nod. "For your brother?" I nod again.

She resumes her knitting, but I can feel her watching me out of the corners of her eyes. I wish I knew what she is thinking. She doesn't seem horrified by my attempt at speech. And Mother need never know about it.

"You must come see me often, Judith," Maria says. "I can see that it will grow lonely sometimes, especially when Leon improves and can be up and about his work all day." She looked around her cottage with satisfaction. "As mistress of my own home, I can invite anyone I choose. So please come see me often, Judith. Come tomorrow. Promise you will."

She wants me back. Surely she could invite any young wife or grown maiden in town to assuage her loneliness. She is watching for my answer. I nod.

She smiles, and we work side by side with our needles for most of another hour.

LIX.

I all but skip home. A friendly wind is at my back, and my feet feel light over the beaten track.

One friend. Do I truly have one friend?

It may be a small social circle, but one friend, to me, feels like bounty.

I can't find a good reason why she would choose me, but I do not doubt her sincerity.

She likes me. She wants me to come back. I don't want to tempt fate by demanding to know why. Only pretty and well-to-do Maria Johnson, now Cartwright, can risk association with me.

But what do I have to offer her? Mine is silent company. I can listen, at any rate.

Maybe it is more what she does not see. My missing tongue does not bother her, and she is stubbornly indifferent to what others think of my reputation.

Take away my missing tongue, and the sins that I did not commit. Why am I not then as likely a friend as any other human soul?

LX.

Back home, Mother works at the cider press. She doesn't need my help, so I sit inside with Darrel and keep working on his book bag. He is seated at the table while the last afternoon light still streams inside, poring over the Bible, the largest book we own. This pleases me. I'm glad he wants to return to school.

I sit down next to him and watch him peering over the page, tracing a line of words with his finger. I look at the black type on the faded yellow paper. I know my letters, and I can sound out simple words, but Darrel delves deeper into the mysteries of words and meanings.

I elbow him.

"What?" He is annoyed with me.

I point to my mouth. To his mouth. To the words on the page. To my ear.

"You want me to read to you?"

Yes, idiot. Read to me.

He shrugs and begins to read. His voice is strong and sure, like the preacher's. Not for nothing, I see, does Mr. Gillis praise his recitation. But when Darrel reads them, unlike Reverend Frye, the words are full of longing, not judgment.

"I will lift up mine eyes unto the hills, from whence cometh my help. My help cometh from the Lord, which made heaven and earth. He will not suffer thy foot to be moved."

Darrel's voice wavers on *foot*. I lower my sewing and watch him. He swallows and forges onward, angry and determined.

"He that keepeth thee will not slumber. Behold, he that keepeth Israel shall neither slumber nor sleep."

He pauses and looks at me. His eyes are wet.

"You went into the hills to bring us help, didn't you, Judith?"

I gaze at him. How does he know? How did he know Phantom was mine now?

He turns back to the book. "The Lord is thy keeper: the Lord is thy shade upon thy right hand. The sun shall not smite thee by day, nor the moon by night. . . ."

LXI.

Later, Darrel rests on his bed, while Mother measures out flour for tomorrow's baking. I sit at the table, and by the light of a candle left burning there, I flip over several leaves, inhaling the musty paper smell, and trace my finger over a wide page of type.

B, y. By. T, h, e, the. By the. R, i, v, e, r, s. Riv, ers. Rivers. By the rivers.

At this rate it will take me a week to finish one passage. But something caught hold of me when Darrel read his words, about the sun and the moon and the hills. I saw pictures, I saw colors, I felt desire. I want to see and feel them again. Even if I can't pronounce them in a voice like his, I can hear the words in my mind.

By the rivers, o, f. Of. By the rivers of.

The next word is long and daunting. *B, a, b, y. Baby? By the rivers of baby? L, o, n. Lon. Baby and lon. Baby-lon.* Then my mind supplies the answer, a word I've heard hundreds of times from the pulpit. Not *baby*, but *babby. Babylon.* City of captivity and sin.

By the rivers of Babylon. What happened there?

I will have to learn later, for Mother turns to wonder at what I'm doing. I glide away from the Bible and outdoors to the barn.

LXII.

Next morning, I rise early and have another go at the passage while Mother dresses herself.

By the rivers of Babylon, I read, feeling rather proud. *T, h, e, r, e. Th,* I remember, makes its own sound, much like the one my half tongue makes whenever I've privately tried to make a *T* sound. *Theer? There. W, e, we. There we. S, a, t, sat.* It's starting to feel easier. *There we sat. By the rivers of Babylon, there we sat, d, o, w, n. Do-uhn? Doon? Down.*

Some words put up more of a fight. *By the rivers of Babylon, there we sat down.*

By the rivers of Babylon, there we sat down.

I look up to see Darrel watching me from bed, under heavy-lidded eyes.

Mother's footstep stirs, and I reach for my dress and petticoats.

LXIII.

That afternoon I return to Maria's. I pass by your house on my way into town, and I don't even look, much, to see if you're about. I have others to think of besides you.

Maria receives me gladly. After more tea and bread with preserves, we sit stitching for some time.

Then she unleashes a thunderbolt.

"Why don't you speak, Judith?"

My needle halts. I turn to look at her. Can she really be asking me this?

Her eyes search my face. "You can, can't you? Somewhat? You said 'book' yesterday. Have you tried to say more?"

All I can feel is my heart pounding, and my mother's warnings, and the dread of increasing the shame I already bear with my hideous sounds.

"Please don't be angry with me," she says. "I've been thinking about this a great deal. We need to find a way for you to talk."

I abandon any thought of stitching. I purse my lips carefully around this sound. My voice cracks, like a sick person's does.

"Why?"

Maria's eyebrows rise in triumph. She reaches for my hand.

"Because I want to know you," she says. "And others will want to as well."

I feel perspiration rise beneath my shift. The sheer effort of such an explanation as I must now make is more, even, than when I tried to talk to the colonel.

"*They . . . sshay . . .*" I must think hard about each sound, how each muscle of my face and throat might now combine to form it. Years offer plenty of time to forget. "*. . . I'hm . . . curshedth.*"

Maria pours me a cup of tea, and I hide my mouth behind it gratefully.

"I know some say you're cursed," she says quietly. "Tell them otherwise."

LXIV.

Walking home that afternoon, I practice quiet, little sounds that barely escape my mouth. *Mmah, mmoo, mmee, mmay, mmoh. Bah, boh, bee, bah, buh. Puh, poh, pih, pah.* My lips are thinking hard about each try.

She's half deaf, but even so I feel exposed when I come around a bend and encounter Goody Pruett hobbling along the path with an empty basket bumping against her hip.

"You're out and about a good deal more lately, Miss Judith," she observes, watching me sideways through her dark eyes. She taps her chin with a bent finger. "Now, what might you be up to?"

I pause and breathe while trying to think. I have as much

right as anyone to walk this path. But she's rattled me, for as ever she has seen right through me.

"You ever need something, you know how to find me," she says. "You could do worse than to look to Goody Pruett for help."

Lacking anything else to say to this, I curtsy. I don't need help. She means well, and I like Goody well enough. At least she's not afraid of me. But even if I could tell her something, I'd never trust secrets to that old gossip.

LXV.

By the rivers of Babylon, there we sat down, yea, we wept, when we remembered Zion.

I have wept by a river for my homeland, too. A stream, more like. When I crossed it coming home after my years away.

We hanged our harps upon the willows in the midst thereof.

I have no harp, but I hung memories of Lottie and of a happy childhood in my willow by the river.

LXVI.

"With Darrel an invalid like he is now," Mother says to me, "you know there's more work than the both of us can manage. So I don't know what call you have to be sneaking off to stare at a book when you can't read anyway."

LXVII.

"I've been doing some practicing," Maria says at the next

day's visit. "Don't laugh—I've been experimenting to see what sounds can be made without . . . a tongue. There's—as I said, there's no reason to dillydally about the truth, is there? Without a tongue. Do you lack all of your tongue, or only some? Open your mouth for me."

I've never encountered such a person, but by now I've grown used to her. I open my mouth and thrust forward what remains of my tongue. Too late I feel shy of my breath, my teeth.

She reaches forward and takes my jaw in her hands, tilting my head to angle it toward the light coming in from the window. She studies me like a doctor might, with eager curiosity and no sign of horror.

"There," she said. "I believe you can regain at least some speech. And with practice, you can have a way to be understood. That would make all the difference, wouldn't it? All the difference in the world?"

I don't know how to feel. I am weary of having to choose my facial expressions the way others can choose their words. For those who wish to read my face, every movement on its surface becomes my shout. As with Abijah Pratt the other day, my only protection is stillness.

I push slowly and awkwardly through my answer. *"I wonth everh shoun gootth."*

She searches my face, her eyes darting back and forth. Even she couldn't understand me this time. Then she nods. She has it.

"Who is to say that you won't ever sound good?"

I tap my own breastbone angrily. I say so. And so would

anyone else who values how elegant speech can and should sound.

"I think you should try. With practice, you can improve." Her eyes lit up. "Leon and I visited with the Aldruses last night. They have the two little ones, of course, and I watched the youngest as she tried to speak. Her mother corrects her, and so she learns, and she will improve in time. Why not you?"

I hang my head. I am torn between desire to speak—to be heard, to one day speak to you—and despair. I will always sound like ruin, a destroyed voice, a broken mouth. Why not me? Because the little Aldrus baby has a round, pink tongue.

Maria clasps my hands. "You're safe here, Judith," she says. "Just try it. Please. Will you?"

Now I know why you could not—cannot, for all I know— resist her. She could coax honeybees out of their nests.

I open my eyes to hers, without my stillness veiling them. I nod.

She rubs her hands together. "Say something. Make any sound you can. Say 'ah.'"

I feel self-conscious. I swallow to moisten my throat. "Ah." I sound like someone with whooping cough.

"That's right! Say it again. 'Ah. Ah. Ah.'"

I oblige her.

"Slowly. 'Aaaaahhh.'"

I say it slowly.

"There, now that's better. You have a lovely sound. Don't wag your eyes at me, I mean it. Now, try 'oh.'"

She drags me through all kinds of sounds, soft sounds

needing no tongue, harsh ones that can be made with lips, guttural ones that can be formed in the back of my throat. *Mm. Wa. Ff. Ba. Ha. Pa. Err. Va. Gg. Ck. Ng.* My lips are weary from the exertion. My throat is dry and tired.

Maria, however, is triumphant. She thrusts out her arms. "See what you can do?"

Her pleasure in me warms me. *"Yesh,"* I say. *"Yesh, Maria."*

She jumps up and embraces me. Then Leon hobbles through the door on his crutches and wonders at us.

When I finally go home, I realize from the darkening skies that I've been there for almost two hours. Mother will be fit to be tied. My throat is tired. My tongue, such as it is, is sore from stretching. My steps are triumphant. I have a friend. When I spoke to her, I did not frighten her. I spoke her name, because she first spoke mine.

LXVIII.

Halfway home, almost to your house, I risk humming a tune. I don't even need to open my mouth for that. The melody bounces in keeping with my step. It buzzes, tingling the roof of my mouth.

I stop. Someone is following me. I'm certain of it. I venture on, then I stop again, and the footsteps stop, but when I resume there they are again. Loud enough to know they're not trying to go unnoticed, yet when I look around, there is no one to be seen.

I shouldn't have hummed. I increase my pace. Must be one of the older middling boys from the school. Darrel's old classmates. Mather, maybe, or Hoss. Baiting the village mute is good sport, for she can never tell tales to your pa.

LXIX.

Evening chores, and I talk to Phantom and Person. First I practice the sounds. *Gg. Ck. Ff.* "*Good cow,*" I can say. "*Phanhom.*"

They look at me strangely and shove at me with their noses. I laugh out loud.

LXX.

Mother retires to bed, but Darrel stays up to read, and I sit up stitching his bag by the shared candlelight. When Mother is fully settled down for the night, Darrel wordlessly slides the Bible over to me. He even knows what page I am on.

We exchange a silent look. Then he watches me read. He will not tell.

LXXI.

By the rivers of Babylon, there we sat down, yea, we wept, when we remembered Zion. We hanged our harps upon the willows in the midst thereof.

For there they that carried us away captive required of us a song; and they that wasted us required of us mirth, saying, Sing us one of the songs of Zion.

How shall we sing the Lord's song in a strange land?

I cry for the captives and their broken hearts hanging tangled in their harps in the willows by the riverside.

LXXII.

In the early morning, I rise before my chores need doing and walk out far into the woods, over crackling pathways of fallen leaves, to Father's rock. The sky is purple, the sun only just peeking over the horizon. I look around; I am utterly alone.

I stand on the rock, close my eyes, and sing.

I sing a wordless song, ahs and ohs, to the melody of an old tune that Father taught me years ago.

At first the sound embarrasses me, and I peek around as if the trees might criticize. I squeak, I crackle. I run out of air before the sound has even begun. I swallow and breathe deeply and try again. Softly, softly. A little better now.

Let your body rest, Father used to say, when we would sing here. Put your whole body to sleep. Let only the music be awake.

The tune is a little sweeter this time. My breath lasts a little longer. But the cold air chills my throat.

Start slowly, softly. It's almost as if I can hear Father teaching me. He was a fine singer at Sunday meetings. Everyone knew it. We looked to him to carry the tune.

I try yet again. My pleasure in the sound begins to tingle on my skin.

I close my eyes. I try to imagine my body asleep, with only the musical air rushing out and in. Again and again I sing, until the sound is limber, light, and pure. What is this thing inside me that can make such sound, after so long? How could I have let it be stilled?

I sing with my arms open wide, my eyes watching as the tree limbs stir in the morning breeze. My voice is nothing like my little-girl voice.

I sing a new melody, one that climbs higher. I remember the words, even though I don't try them yet, for I want nothing to mar this moment.

O Love, in the Spring, thou art wondrous fair,
O Love, let down thy golden hair!
O Love, in the Spring, will you marry me?
O Love, will you always my true love be?

At last, I must stop. My throat grows tired again. I must do this more, when I can get away. I jump down from the rock that has become my stage and turn back to the path that will lead me home.

I find you standing on the path, watching me.

I clap my hand over my mouth and close my eyes.

When I open them you are still there, caught in the sunrise, looking at me like I'm someone else.

I hurry past you and run for home.

LXXIII.

Morning chores are torture. I'm clumsy and slow; I keep forgetting what I should be doing. I fumble an egg and drop it on my boot, I bring in overnight logs instead of kindling. Mother grumbles, but I barely hear her.

At breakfast I spread butter on both sides of my bread, and Mother squawks again. Darrel laughs out loud. It's the first we've heard that sound in a long time.

My head is full of audacity: Maria's teaching me to speak. My head is full of song, of notes that chime in my teeth. *O Love, will you always my true love be?*

My head is full of seeing you see me.

LXXIV.

There is a knock at the door.

Mother wipes her hands on her apron and settles her cap between her fingertips. She squares her shoulders and pulls the door back. Light washes over her face and form, as if she's greeting a heavenly messenger.

Your voice speaks.

"Good morning, Mrs. Finch," you say.

Mother bobs her head in the smallest of curtsies. "Mr. Whiting."

I inch toward the wall, to be more in the door's shadow and to catch sight of you through the gap.

"How is Darrel?"

Mother presses her lips together and says nothing. Grace for grace, Mother, for heaven's sake. After all you've done for us! I cringe at her rudeness.

And then you say, "I wonder if I might have a private word with your daughter?"

LXXV.

There is only the sound of sun shining through the door.

If I had a proper tongue it would be dry as salt.

LXXVI.

Without moving, Mother's back becomes a stake.

"A *word* with my daughter?" The slant on *word* is slight, yet its sarcasm stings. At our mothers' knees we learn the music that turns words into kisses or curses.

Mother throws the door back toward the wall. I jump aside to avoid being struck.

"Come in," she says indifferently. "She's right here." Nodding toward me, she returns to the table and her bucket of bloodstained bandages. She stirs them with a paddle and lifts them to drip.

Heart of mine, don't fail me now.

You step inside.

You must stoop to pass through the doorway. Once inside, you straighten to your full height and fill the entire room. Your hat dangles in your hand, lined with the sweat of your face.

I make myself stand straight like Mother. I make myself step forward. But I can't make myself reach out my hand to touch yours. Not with her here.

"I had hoped for a private conversation." You speak to my mother but your eyes are on me.

"Secrets are as safe with me as they are with her." Mother stirs Darrel's cloths like soup. "Whatever you want to say, you can say right here."

I could throttle my mother. I fear I may burst. Here you stand, come to call on me. Does it show that I'm shaking?

You look troubled, anxious, torn. How can you be unsure of yourself? If I were you I'd spend every moment reveling in my own skin. But apparently neither the trim of your thigh nor the brawn of your chest can help whatever troubles you.

You rotate your hat brim between your hands.

"Good morning to you both," you say, and turn and walk away.

I call after you. *"Wai-!"*

Mother slams the door and glowers at me.

LXXVII.

Through the window I watch you disappear. You walk slowly,

like one arrested by his thoughts, and once you pause. Will you come back?

You don't. I press my face against the cold, damp glass.

"Don't be chasing after him." Mother lets a lump of rags splash back into her pail.

That's all she says to me for the rest of the day.

LXXVIII.

It takes her an eternity to fall asleep that night. She won't even go to bed until well past midnight. I close my eyes and pretend to breathe like a sleeper, and this is dangerous, for such subterfuge has more than once tricked me into real sleep while I waited for Mother to succumb. But nothing could lull me tonight, not while I know that you've come for me, not after an entire day of maddening speculation. Such torture, and yet so sweet—the wondering why—I can barely bring myself to pity Darrel. Who could be afflicted when I feel so alive?

At last her breathing slows, becomes a regular rhythm. Still I wait. I am good at waiting, though tonight every nerve in my body wants to burst out of my skin.

The room is black as iron. Cold night air seeps through the window near my bed. Darrel moans in his sleep. Outside coyotes bark.

I rise from my bed and pause to see if Mother stirs. She doesn't.

I lace on my shoes and cover myself with a coat. Mother is past knowing what I do.

The door will betray me if anything can. I feel around it,

up and down, and in its path. Mother has left a pan of dry beans on the floor before the door. A trap.

I am eighteen. Old enough to be married and keeping a house of my own. If she is so ashamed of me, why does she want to keep me here forever? Not for love of my company.

I inch away the pan of beans. I take an hour, or so it feels, to lift the latch and coax the door open. I step out into the night breezes that whip through my long hair. It's wicked of me to go see you without my cap, with my hair down. I'm drunk with the thought of it.

I close the door and take my first soft steps. As soon as I'm past hearing, my feet run to you. They know the way. The dark night hides my errand. Branches brush my face. My hair flows behind me like a banner waving. I feel myself swelling, bursting with this moment and my daring. The night in the woods was nothing to this. All the while it's you who fills my thoughts, you who have come asking for me, you who thought of me, why I don't know, but if you but think of me I'll fly to you.

LXXIX.

Your house appears. I stop. Breathing is painful. There's a light in your window.

The door is dark, but a line shines underneath, pulling me like a moth.

This is why I've come, and I can't go back until I know what you wanted to say to me.

How will I answer you, when you speak to me? Will my sounds revolt you?

You know I can't speak. I trust you. You are the kindest person I know. My heart is in your hands.

I will my feet to carry me to your door.

I raise my hand and knock.

LXXX.

Footsteps. Latch. And there you are. Your shirt unbuttoned halfway down, your hair rumpled, your lips parted, your eyes shocked.

I hug my arms around myself and curse myself back to my bed.

But there you stand, haloed by lamplight, every warm, shining inch of you. You take in my hair, the scandalous bridal white of my nightdress. Do I imagine, or do you look at me in a way you've never done before?

"Judith."

My name, again, from you. We are not on the public street tonight.

Your eyes are wide; this is so improper. But it's the middle of the night, and no one is about to see. You hold your door wide. "Please, come in."

I walk in, invited this time. I'm not sure what to do next, but you offer me a chair, then swing your kettle back over the fire and throw another stick on the flames. I'm to be offered a drink, a cup of tea. I sit up straighter in my chair.

You sit down opposite me and bend forward. I can see into your shirt, and it flushes me with heat. You search my face, which seems to make you unsure of yourself, and so your eyes rest on my hair.

"It was good of you to come."

The village would not agree, but we shall let the error pass.

I don't want to stare at you and add to your unease, so I look around the cottage. It's dark, save for the firelight and a lamp on the table. The bed with its blue-patterned spread fills my vision. Not long ago, I draped that blanket over you.

"You must think me strange."

Oh no! I shake my head. Not you. Never.

"May I ask you a question?"

Of course.

"It's just that, for all these years, I never thought I'd . . ."

I'm leaning toward you, staring at your teeth, your lips, your red tongue as you speak. You rake your fingers through your hair, looking like you've just rolled from bed. I don't know how I'm breathing.

You speak to the floor. "I have to know, before I go mad," you whisper. "Was it . . ."

I reach forward and touch your hand. Twice now. Such fire under dry leather skin. I squeeze it and force you to look into my eyes. What do you see? You can ask me anything, Lucas, and I'll answer with all the truth that's in me, even if I have to draw my foolish pictures to do it. There's nothing I wouldn't tell you, if I could, and if you asked me. Nothing I wouldn't do.

You struggle to swallow, as if there's a bone in your throat. Your eyes are fixed upon my hand holding yours. When you look back at me, you're pleading and my heart breaks for you. I don't relinquish your hand.

"You brought my father to the battle and saved us all."

I bask in pleasure, even though you've brought him into the room.

"After all these years of thinking he was dead, it was a shock to see him alive. I've been tortured by the thought. . . . So many thoughts: why didn't he come to me, why wouldn't he let me help him, didn't he want to see me?"

He hurt so many people. Of course you suffered. But you did a brave job of hiding it. And here you are, confiding your feelings to me, to me!

"But the worst of all is thinking, and fearing . . . I don't want to harrow you, but I fear if I don't know I'll never have a moment's peace in this life again. . . ."

I move my chair an inch closer and look into your eyes with all the reassurance I can.

You lift your head and meet my gaze.

"Was it my father who hurt you?"

LXXXI.

I pull my hands away.

LXXXII.

To say nothing is an answer of a kind.

To answer is another.

To lie could protect you. Would you believe what you wanted to?

To tell the truth will make me loathsome in your eyes. Even more than I already am.

I pledged to give you all the truth that's in me.

And you want me to tell you this.

LXXXIII.

Worse than all else, this was your only purpose in seeking me. And I am the worst of fools.

LXXXIV.

There is desperation in your eyes, and anguish. Desire, and terrible, terrible fear. I have seen that look before. Not in this room, not in your eyes.

Candlelight moves across your face and unveils him before me.

LXXXV.

"Or did he find you," you say, your eyes pleading, "and tend your wounds?"

LXXXVI.

He did find me. He did tend my wounds.

LXXXVII.

Lucas. At your bidding I'd have fallen at your feet. I'd have lied for you, I'd have lied to please you, if I had the words to do it.

But I can't answer you this. Not even for you. In time the truth would make you hate me, if you don't already. But more than that, against all reason, I hold myself too dear.

You want me to tell. You wish to understand your father's sins, to relieve your anguish, even at my expense. To relieve another man's suffering must I expose myself again?

I scrape a tear from my eye. It was not my wish that you see it. But see you have, and your eyes betray you: guilt is settling down upon you, and horror at what you've said.

That can't bring me any comfort.

You hold me in your anguished gaze. Something like realization dawns on your face.

I rise and turn and leave you.

LXXXVIII.

You call after me, after *Judith*, to wait. I don't.

My feet carry me homeward, though I scarcely care if they do or don't. No one at home needs to see my tears nor hear my sobs. The night wind penetrates me. Has it grown colder since I walked here, or is that only my affection?

I think I hear footsteps again, and then I'm sure that I do. It must be you, coming to try to apologize. I walk faster, then run, until I reach my door. I want none of your gallantry now.

Fool to imagine! Fool to dream! Fool to think your visit meant that by some miracle, you might, in spite of everything, come to look on me!

It's enough to know I don't matter to anyone else in the world, but you treated me gently. You made me think you respected me. You let me imagine that you of all men weren't fascinated by what might have happened to me.

That won't excuse me for presuming to give my heart to you. It's not your fault you broke it.

LXXXIX.

I'll go live in the colonel's house. I'll keep my promise to the dead and take no harm from it. Phantom and I will keep each other company. I'll be rid of Mother's contempt, and spared from ever seeing the knowledge in your eyes of how I shamed myself before you, and how your father marred me forever.

For though I will not answer you, I know that I already have.

BOOK THREE

I.

I let the door slam behind me as I go inside. Mother and Darrel thrash around in their sheets and sit up.

"*Mmm,*" I tell them, so they know it's me.

Darrel lies down again. For a long time Mother doesn't move—I can tell from the silence—but at last she lies down.

I get out of my coat and boots and crawl back under my blankets.

Darrel begins to snore.

My body is heavy and sore with grief. Sleep would be welcome, but I can't rest. The silence and blackness smother me, make me want to bolt back out the door and run for the colonel's house across the river tonight. But that's ridiculous.

I will go, though, and when I do, I will learn to stop remembering you.

I have a widow's claim on whatever your father left behind. His hut was the place where young Judith died, and I was born. Ought I not to return to my home?

Young Judith was infatuated with you. I ought to know better.

The night drags on.

"Think he'll marry you?"

Mother. My muscles clench.

"This man of yours. Or boy. The one you keep going to."

I am paralyzed. She thinks I'm bedding a lover in a village hay barn. My own mother.

Her voice is calm and low. From behind her bed curtains, it has a distant, ghostly sound.

"Or is he someone already married?" She could be a friend whispering to me in church.

Can I pretend I'm asleep? No, she knows I'm awake.

"If you're going to make a strumpet of yourself, find another place to live."

I can't even let myself breathe freely, lest my throat reveal some emotion she can seize upon.

"So for your sake," she says, "I hope he can and does marry you."

II.

I learned, during the years with him, how to cry without making a sound. Mostly I learned how to not cry.

But my mother has found a fragment of my feelings that I didn't know was there, and pierced it between her thumb and fingernail.

For her to see me every day, and believe this of me, hurts in my deepest inner parts, wounds wordless memories that I still hold of my life and my mother, before he took and cut me.

III.

I can't live here anymore.

Then I remember, I wasn't planning to. I'm going to move to the colonel's cabin. I'll go tomorrow. Mother is not the reason for my leaving. You are. I leave you both behind.

There is a curious comfort in letting go. After the agony, letting go brings numbness, and after the numbness, clarity. As if I can see the world for the first time, and my place in it, independent of you, a whole vista of what may be. Even if it is not grand or inspiring, it is real and solid, unlike the fantasy I've built around you.

I will do this. I will triumph over you.

IV.

"Wake up, slugabed," Mother barks in my ear. "Winter's come and morning's wasting."

I sit up in bed, disoriented. When did I fall asleep? Did I really go to your house last night? Did Mother really talk to me? She seems her usual self today; did I dream she spit me out?

The sun is indeed already up, and its light is different today. The wood of our cabin walls and doors seems paler, newer.

I look out the window.

Snow! Heavy and deep, and still falling fast.

That explains the strange light, and the muffling quiet that kept me sleeping longer. Even sunrise slipped by unnoticed, absorbed by a foot of snow.

Mother opens a trunk full of winter things—hats and gloves and scarves. I wrap myself up, seize my bucket, and head for the barn. Person will have noticed her morning milk, snowfall or no.

I pitch hay for her and for Phantom, milk Person dry, then clean their stalls. My footprints from coming to the barn are nearly hidden when I return. I squint against driving snowflakes and relentless white to look at the woodpile and the chicken coop. How many days' wood have we laid by? Not enough, if the storm is long. This used to be Darrel's task.

But why should it matter to me whether Mother has enough wood? I'm not staying.

I give Mother the milk, then wade to the chickens. My ankles are wet, the snow biting. I open the hatch, and the hens have sense enough to stay in. I feed and water them quickly, gather the eggs, then rake out the coop and leave the mess where it lands. Snow will bury the odor.

I reach the house and find the door locked. I knock and rattle it with no success. I pound the door, and finally Mother comes. She offers no explanation.

I don't need one.

V.

I peel my wet things off and drape myself over the fire. Darrel edges his chair aside with difficulty to make room for me.

Last night's grandiose plans are a handful of snow down the back of my neck. In this storm I could barely even reach the cabin, much less survive there. Even if this snow were gone in two days, I'm not prepared to venture off alone yet. What would I eat? What would I burn?

And how can I leave Darrel?

But, oh, to endure a winter cooped inside with Mother's scorn.

And you.

I will leave, but not until spring.

VI.

Darrel's face is plastered to the window. He takes a child's delight in the snow. He must wipe the pane each time it frosts over with his breath.

From indoors, where the fire crackles, it is a gorgeous snowfall, coating every branch and limb, painting over autumn's drab with purity. I remember past snows that charmed me just as Darrel is charmed today.

Has he yet considered how the snow will hamper him? Or how he'll even move at all?

"Take me out in it, Judy," he says. "I haven't been outdoors in weeks. I want to taste the snowflakes."

Mother doesn't suppose this even deserves an answer.

Time, then, for Darrel's first outing.

She mashes her hands into her hips when she finds me, moments later, fishing through the trunk for his hat and scarf.

"And what do you think you're doing?"

I hand Darrel his trousers and help him slide them on under his nightshirt. I pull a sock over his stump, then wrap the leg of his trousers up over it and tie a string loosely around it. He pulls on his jacket and bundles his hands and head.

"You're not going out," Mother fumes. "You'll catch your death."

"I lost a foot, not a lung," Darrel says. "It's time for me to see the world again."

"I forbid it."

Darrel reaches out to me and I help him to stand.

His good leg is weak and wobbly. He clings tightly to my

shoulder and I hold on tight to his waist. Together we hop-step, hop-step over the threshold and out into the snow.

"Slip and fall, why don't you, and break your other leg." Mother slams the door behind us.

"Winter always did cheer her up," says Darrel.

He breathes deeply, filling himself with winter air. It smells clean and moist and sweet. His eyes are not accustomed to so much light after lying so long in the dark house, and he squints. Snowflakes melt into his orange lashes.

I look out across the way toward the stream, which snarls like long black lips across the white face of the earth. Beyond, out of sight, is your house. I see a column of smoke rise through the white sky, loose and unfurling like a girl's long hair without her cap.

What are you about today?

Why do I care?

I don't.

This will be a new amputation. You've been a part of my flesh, underneath all my skin. Your removal will bleed and leave me lame for a time.

VII.

I nudge Darrel and we hop forward. Snow squeaks under our feet. Once his leg seems to falter under his weight, and I pull him against me. He's skin and bones now, and only a bit taller than me, so it's not difficult to support him.

"Bet Mather and Hoss'll be sledding at Drummond's Hill," Darrel says.

I nod. Undoubtedly they and a dozen other schoolboys will be there today after morning chores are done.

"Class'd be cancelled, anyhow."

His teeth chatter slightly. I'm not cold yet; the poor goose hasn't enough meat on him to be out here in such weather.

I try to steer him back, but he refuses to budge. If I try to force him I'll knock him headlong into a drift.

He looks at my face as if he's just now noticed my nose.

"I want to go back to school, Judy," he says. "It's my only chance."

I study his blue-gray eyes. I understand.

"Will you help me get there?"

My thoughts swirl and scatter like snowflakes on an errant wind. Will I help him make something of his life? Who will help me? Why does everyone presume that I, as damaged merchandise, forfeit any claim to happiness? That I expect nothing, have no ambitions or longings of my own? When was it agreed that my lot would be to gladly serve as a prop and a crutch for others who are whole?

And what rules of economy dictate that a boy without a foot is more whole than a girl without a tongue?

If I presume that Darrel has even given two seconds' thought to me and my desires, I'm the fool the town supposes I am.

"Whaddya say, Judy?" He grins his dimples at me.

Darrel still thinks about his own future, as he should. And he's right. Mother will do all she can to prevent him going, and without schooling, what can a cripple do?

Not much, as I know well.

But if I promise to help him, it locks me here, where you will always be nearby to rub salt in my open wounds.

I'm trapped for this winter. Come spring, we'll both be

more able to move. Darrel can walk to school with a crutch, and I can walk away to my new home.

How shall we sing the Lord's song in a strange land?

Could I, by some miracle, find books to take with me to the colonel's cabin? And could I, before winter is over, learn enough to read them?

I won't be Darrel's crutch. I make a decision. If I must stay, my delay will purchase me something useful. I clear my throat.

"*You . . .*" I say. His eyes widen. "*You . . . go. I go. I rea—*" I am struggling with the word. "*Reab,*" it comes out.

"Judy!"

His face is all astonishment. It has been many, many years since Darrel heard my voice.

"*I wan tho reab.*" I try again. "*Readth.*" I pull the stump of my tongue forward. "*Wlearn to readth. You heowp me . . . wlearn . . . to . . . readth.*" Each word demands my total concentration.

Darrel blinks like he's seen a heavenly messenger. "You want me to help you learn to read." He's immensely proud of himself. My brother, the genius. "I've seen you working on it already. But, Judy!" He grins. "Listen to you talk!"

I glare at him. He retreats a bit. "It's a start, anyway. . . . Mother doesn't like you to speak, does she?"

I shake my head, then shrug. Mother's days of making my rules are numbered.

He chews on his lower lip. "She won't like me going to school. Nor me teaching you to read."

I shrug. "*You wan tho go, you heowp me readth.*"

He nods.

I scribble an imaginary pen through the air. *"An wriye."*

"And write."

Yes.

"Can't you write?"

I shake my head.

He nods slowly. "Too long ago to remember much." His eyes are alight. "Here's how we'll do it. You bring me to school, and you stay and listen. You be a student with the other girls. And at home, at night, I'll help you. Agreed?"

Stay at school all day? Away from Mother, away from your house?

"Yesh." To seal the bargain, I toss him over into a snow-drift.

He lands flailing and sputtering and is nearly half buried. His laughter rings out and bounces off the gray bones of forest trees.

VIII.

The snow lets up later in the afternoon. The sun appears in the white sky, and the house, so well insulated by drifts, grows warm and cozy until nightfall. I sit sewing by the fire and remember last night, before the snow. It might have been another world, another century, when I ran across dry leaves to you at midnight, in only a nightgown and coat.

I remember the changing mood in your eyes, and ponder what it meant.

I stab a needle through the dry, tough skin on my knuckle by mistake, and inspect the empty tunnel of white flesh that's left behind when I yank the needle out.

IX.

How shall we sing the Lord's song in a strange land?

If I forget thee, O Jerusalem, let my right hand forget her cunning.

If I do not remember thee, let my tongue cleave to the roof of my mouth; if I prefer not Jerusalem above my chief joy.

X.

The next morning, I go outside, swathed in scarves and shawls and armed with my bucket. It's an effort to push the door open. At last I do, yet I remain rooted to the threshold.

"What's the matter?" Mother calls to me, hurrying over to shut the door behind me.

I point to the ground around our house. It is covered in footprints, in front, in back, at every window. Where the snow piles deep, the prints are troughs, as if someone waded through.

"Lord have mercy," Mother says, then pulls me in and shuts the door.

XI.

"Could be that Whiting boy," Mother says, peering out through a gap in the shuttered window. I make sure my face betrays no emotion. I know from the pigeon-toed prints that it isn't you. But the boots were large, whoever wore them.

"Or someone from the village, stopping by to inquire after us in the evening," Darrel adds.

"Some tramp or other, who's gone on his way by now?" Mother looks to me as if I might have the answer. She thinks it's my lover. I return her gaze.

I hope it's the village boys, in the mood for mischief and nothing more. Though mischief itself can be quite enough where overgrown boys are concerned.

After some time of peering out each window, Mother grows impatient enough with the threat of danger to thrust me out into it. Person must be milked, after all. I stamp my way through the snow, which has a hard crust over it, leaving my footprints crude and unintelligible. Not so for the other footprints, though. They must have been made earlier, when the new snow was still soft and powdery.

XII.

I finish my chores and bring in all the wood I can wrench from the frozen pile. As I work, I repeat the word: *Maria*. *Maria*. It's all in the lips. The R is a bit awkward, but with practice, I can say it just like anyone else would. A listener would never know I wasn't whole. After breakfast, I bundle up once more and strap on Darrel's snowshoes.

"And where do you think you're going?" Mother demands.

"Maria," I say, savoring the way the word sails forth almost as much as watching Mother's cheek twitch.

What can she say to that? There's nothing cursed or devilish about how I say *Maria*.

I step out into the blinding sunlight on the snow.

Walking over the drifts in my snowshoes presents a new aspect of the world, one from three feet higher than usual. It makes me feel giddy, as though I might fall off my perch, even though my perch is everywhere.

From this high up, your house looks humbled and insignificant, engulfed by snow. By habit I glance at the windows for a sign of your whereabouts, until I remember not to.

There's nothing for it but to enjoy my tramp through the snow toward the village. The snowshoes slap onto the crust of snow like hands on a drum. Every bird that swoops from branch to branch adds cheery color and movement to the cold, white stillness.

In town the sight is less pristine, where dozens of men battle with sleds and shovels to claw through the snow then haul it away. I reach Maria's house and find her wrestling with a shovel outside her door. She's not skilled at using it, and she knows it.

"Sorry about this," she says, looking down at her boots. "Leon's not well enough to do it, and I've got to get it done before the snow ices over any more."

"Me," I say, reaching out my hands for the shovel.

She thrusts the blade deep into a drift. "What, 'me'?"

It feels like Mother forcing me to say *please* when I was very young. I'm annoyed with her.

"Me," I repeat, gesturing as if shoveling snow. If she's going to be coy about receiving help, next time I won't be so quick to offer.

"'*Let* me,'" she prompts. "You sound like an imbecile. Use language worthy of your mind. Use what you have. Stretch it forward."

My tongue would need to touch the backs of my teeth for the *L* and the *T* sounds in "let." I know it won't stretch forward that far. I'm angry enough to prove it to her. I thrust the stump of my tongue forward.

"Uueh me," I say, sparing her none of my irritation.

"Excellent!" She beams at me. "I think there was a bit of

T in there. Try it again. Cut the sound off abruptly. Land's sakes, we hardly say half our *T*s as it is."

I am grotesque when I try to engage my tongue, like a drunken idiot. I glance around, but there are no witnesses except the icicles on Maria's roof. I shove my tongue toward my teeth until its sinews ache, and loosen my lips trying to form the sounds.

"Ueh me. Ueh me. Ueht me. Wleht me."

Maria shrieks and points at my mouth. "There, you see! Practice. Practice is all you need. You'll never win an elocution prize, but you can make yourself understood, if you practice. Here, here's the shovel. You've earned it." She tosses the handle toward me with a wink and disappears into her house.

I don't know whether to laugh at Maria or throw down her shovel and trudge back home. Let me. Let me. "Llleht me." It's near enough to an *L* that it couldn't be confused for anything else. I practice the words once more. The *L* improves each time, though it's never as good as hers. The *T* is a bit heavy, a bit moist, as though it has a small *th* at its end, but it serves as a passable *T*.

Maria returns with a second shovel, and I forgive her. "Leht me," I announce.

We fall to shoveling. Snow flies in our faces like flour on baking day.

"See what other *L* words you can say," Maria says.

I consider. I have to concentrate so hard on my tongue stump's movements each time, I fear I may slaver on myself. "Lllap." That was overdone. I wipe my lip and try again. "Low. Laugh." This earns a smile. "Lamb. Lu . . ." I feel my face grow warm despite the sting of cold grains of snow.

Maria gives me a sly wink. "That's all right. You can say his name aloud. It won't bother me any."

With an effort I control my face. That was a narrow miss. "Lu-cash," I say, then shrug, as if you were any other word to me.

"Leonh."

Maria smiles.

XIII.

The sky turns pink, and I bid Maria "goo-bye," at which she applauds. As it happened, we never went indoors, but we cleared her a path to the street, her woodpile, and her shed. I am shy as I kiss her cold, red cheek. She kisses mine. How long has it been since I kissed anyone?

I'm eager to get back. My feet and hands are damp. Passing down the main street, I see Alderman Brown in the doorway of his home, talking with Abijah Pratt, who stands on his porch. Alderman Brown shakes his head yet listens intently to Abijah. When they hear me approach, they turn to look. Neither says anything, but Alderman Brown inclines his head toward me. I hurry to get past them as quickly as I can.

I race against the dropping sun, which bronzes the path before me. I shade my eyes. It seems as though the sun sets right over my mother's house. And, for that matter, yours.

You are going indoors when I pass by, your arms loaded with wood. You drop the wood when you see me and hurry out to where I stand. But you, in your boots, can only walk in the tracks you've dug out, while I skate over the drifts like a water bug on the stream. I look down upon you, and when you look back up at me the setting sun behind me blinds you. Your nose is red and dripping. I wonder if mine is, too.

"Judith," you say. "Please don't go."

I look around for passersby, for the ubiquitous Goody Pruett. Out here in public, you could be fined for calling me by my Christian name. You are safe for today.

You move to one side so the sun is less cruel and look up at me again, scrutinizing me. I'm glad that this time I'm well covered from chin to toe.

You wipe your nose on your coat sleeve and make another attempt. "The other night I . . . I don't know where to begin. . . . I wish I hadn't . . ."

I can wait patiently for many things, but the sun might set before you finish a thought. And I have no wish to revisit that night.

"Yesh?" The *sh* is so slight, it might go unnoticed.

You cock your head so abruptly it's comical. Like a rooster. I want to laugh. This time I surprised you for certain. It makes me feel bold.

"Yesh, Mishder Whidhing?" I'm surprised and pleased at how close I sound to natural. Even in its foreign nature, my speech can be pleasant and warm, through the cadence and music of words. I don't sound brutish. My father's music is in my voice, and not even your father could take that away from me.

You're roostering again. "You talk," you say—rather stupidly, if you'll forgive me.

Yes, I nod. Obviously. You look utterly confounded. I'm enjoying myself.

I rack my brain for the sounds I can and can't make, the

words I can and can't say, searching for the choicest way to end this interview. And then I decide, it doesn't matter anymore. There is no more shame. I no longer dream of pleasing you, so I'll say whatever I wish to say, and what comes out will come out.

I make a small curtsy. "Goodh evenging, Mishder Whidhing," as politely as Maria's own mother might. And without looking back, I walk home toward the lip of the sun that hovers over my mother's snow-shortened roof.

XIV.

I slip away to Sunday meeting, arriving early. Neither Mother nor Darrel goes. Convalescing is still their excuse, though I imagine they will not be able to stretch this pardon out much further. I come because it is the law, but I also come for words to fill my head, and people to observe from my pew in the rear. Not because I yearn for sermons and prayers.

And not because I'm anxious to see you.

Eunice Robinson, on the other hand, clearly has no other objective in mind. At the tolling of the bells, she minces her way down the aisle and into the pew opposite you. She's been pinching her cheeks in the entryway, I can tell. You reward her pains with one of your smiles.

Your hair is groomed to a shine, and your face freshly shaven. The ebony coat you'd had sewn for your wedding is brushed smooth. Shopping for a new bride already? Is it worth enduring more abuse from Leon's relatives?

Not that your doings are of any consequence to me.

The villagers trickle in. The blacksmith, Horace Bron, and his wife, Alice, as small a woman as ever married a giant. The

Cartwrights, senior and junior. The storekeeper, Abe Duddy, and his wife, Hepzibah. The Cavendishes and their six small children. William Salt, the miller, who still wears the black armband for his son, Toby. The Wills, the Robinsons. The pews fill. Sunlight slants through the windows in golden beams, like the morning of Creation.

Rupert Gillis, the slim schoolmaster, is the only one among us who ever studied music, so he leads us in the hymn. Then Preacher Frye, his limp even more pronounced, takes the podium. It seems to me that the silver streak in his hair is whiter than before. He takes his text from the eleventh chapter of Proverbs.

"The integrity of the upright shall guide them: but the perverseness of transgressors shall destroy them. Riches profit not in the day of wrath: but righteousness delivereth from death. The righteousness of the perfect shall direct his way: but the wicked shall fall by his own wickedness."

The room is silent. Not even babies dare to peep. I don't like the way Preacher Frye's eyes linger on you.

"From the Book of Lamentations: 'Our *fathers* have sinned, and are not; and we have borne their iniquities.'"

From where I sit I see only your back. Even so, I see you stiffen.

"Brothers and sisters, we had in our midst a deceiver, a wine-bibber, a man who dabbled in destruction. We believed, years ago, he had gone to his Maker to reap what he had sown."

Oh, Lucas. Go home quickly.

"But he lay hidden away all these years, doing who knows what manner of mischief. Once he was rich, but did his riches profit him in the day of wrath? He appeared at the battle, and as the Scripture says, the wicked fell by his own wickedness. His perverseness has destroyed him. Be not misled into calling this man a hero."

I am sick for you; I fear I will be physically sick for you.

"Thus saith the Preacher in the book of Ecclesiastes, 'For God shall bring every work into judgment, with every secret thing, whether it be good, or whether it be evil.'"

A late entrant opens the rear door, and a chill wind curls around the chapel. I feel it sharply on my sweating face. It is only Goody Pruett.

"Have we not found the answer to so many of our questions? Has the Lord not revealed to us the evil that has vexed us all these years? Thefts. Torments. Young lives taken. Altered forever." Preacher Frye's eyes rest on me. "There are no secrets in the eyes of God. He shouts the deeds of sinful men from the rooftops.

"Now, some among you will say, 'Yes, Preacher Frye, but didn't that man Ezra Whiting come and win the war for us? So it would seem. But listen, and I'll tell you the word of the Lord on the subject.

"The Psalmist said it: 'Thou calledst in trouble, and I delivered thee; I answered thee in the secret place of thunder: I proved thee at the waters of Meribah.'"

He slaps the open pages of the large church Bible.

"Women and families, were we not praying for deliverance? Men of Roswell Station, was it not a place of thunder? Was not the river our own 'waters of Meribah'? Were we not tested and proved there to see if our faith would hold?

"It was the Lord who fought our battles for us. Not a

sinner whom the Lord used as a tool in his hands, then sent
to his eternal judgment. Make no mistake. Woe unto them
who call good evil and evil good. And woe unto those that
harbor iniquity in their families, for the Lord God visiteth
the sins of the fathers upon the children, and the children's
children, to the third and the fourth generation."

Eunice shifts herself in her seat, angling her face away
from you. You don't fail to notice.

Reverend Frye goes on in this fashion for another half an
hour, intones a prayer, and sits down. Rupert Gillis stands
for another hymn, a halfhearted affair. More eyes are on
your back than on the schoolmaster's arm.

After the song, people rise to leave, but you stay rooted to
your pew. The congregation lingers in the rear of the chapel,
swapping conversation and dreading the wet snow.

Reverend Frye makes his way down the aisle toward you.
Seeing him, you rise and stride down the aisle of the church,
your Sunday coattails flapping behind you. Your gaze sweeps
over Eunice's bonnet, and I see a trace of sorrow. Yet another
village belle you've lost. You see me, too, and press your
lips together. Perhaps you know that I alone can empathize
today. You push your way through the gossipers and leave.
The others flow out after you and linger on the stoop.

"Lucas," Alderman Brown calls out from the porch.
"What ails you?"

You turn. Your face is livid. Even inside the church I can
hear your answer.

"Did we risk our lives to defend a just society, where guilt
must be proven and not assumed? Or are we no better than
the oppressive kings from whom our fathers fled?"

I look over to where Reverend Frye leans on his cane in the doorway. He and I are the only ones left inside the church. He glances over and notices me, then returns to the podium to gather his things.

XV.

The breeze is warm and the sunshine bright on my way home from church. The snow turns wet and heavy but still has days of melting left. Chances are tonight the cold will strengthen and I'll wake up to a sheet of ice.

I stomp my way through the thick mush, taking a child's pleasure in it, in spite of everything.

Maria wasn't in church this morning. Leon told me when I passed by him that she was feeling poorly today. He made a point of telling the preacher, too. I am sorry for her but pleased that Leon acknowledged me as his wife's friend. I wonder if our shoveling had exhausted her. She wasn't raised for hard work.

I pass by your house, and Jip comes flopping through the snow to sniff me and paw at my skirts. The poor old thing can't smell, but habits last longer than senses. I squat down to pet him.

"Sshorry, boy," I say, feeling wonderfully free with a deaf dog. "I haven't gotth anything." Better on the Ns! I scratch between his ears and he squinches his eyes with pleasure. "Good boy," I croon. "Good boy." It sounds more like "goo boy."

The sun is high overhead, and my stomach rumbles for its dinner. I pat Jip one last time and stand up. Just in time I

see you move away from your front window, but not without
seeing torment on your face.

Poor Lucas. No one wants to see a neighbor publicly
shamed at meeting. If I could, I would read you Darrel's
book about the French girl. There's a lesson in it for would-
be heroes. The people you save won't celebrate you. They'll
gather the wood and cheer while you burn.

XVI.

I can hear them arguing before I reach the door. I linger outside for a few moments to survey the battle.

"I will too go!" Darrel yells. "Why shouldn't I?"

"You'll slip and fall and break your neck." Mother is
slamming pots and trenchers around by the sound of things.

"Then that would be one less thing for you to worry
about."

"Don't talk that way."

"I'm no good like this. With schooling I could do something. Provide for myself. If I sit here, I'll rot. If I die trying
to better myself, so be it."

"That's fools' talk. You think I can bear to see something
worse befall you?" Mother's voice has dropped, and I have to
press my ear against the door to hear her.

Darrel doesn't answer.

"You're my only son." Mother's voice is gentle, cajoling.

There is a small silence.

"What about Judith?" Darrel says. "She's your only
daughter."

Mother thumps her bowls some more. I feel a sinking

dread in my stomach at what she might or might not say.

"We weren't talking about her," Mother says. "We were talking about you."

My first thought is to slip away to the barn. My second thought is the one I follow.

I open the door and walk in.

Mother avoids my gaze.

XVII.

We pass a strained and silent afternoon. School isn't mentioned again. After eating and chores, we all go to bed early.

In the morning I wake before Mother and tend to all my chores well before the sun is up. I pack a pail with some food for our lunch and hide it in a corner. I build the fire and heat water for breakfast, and I help Darrel dress himself. I try to do all that I would be expected to do during the day so she can have little occasion to complain.

Mother appears and watches us warily, eyeing us for a telling move, like a cat waiting for a mouse to bolt. But as the kettle is singing and the table spread for breakfast, with both of us dressed and seated, there is little she can say.

After we eat, as if by silent understanding, Darrel stands with his crutch and hobbles over toward where the coats hang by the door. He's concealed his books and his broken slate in a strap inside one sleeve—he must have done it in the night. Clever Darrel! I wrap myself in scarves and a coat, take the lunch pail, and offer Darrel my arm.

Mother is silent. A cat about to pounce.

I open the door, and we go outside into the silvered snow. The sky is pale, and our breath freezes in puffs. Neither of us looks back. That's all Mother would need to stop us.

I lean Darrel against the side of the house. "Wait here," I tell him. As I suspected, the melted snow froze in the night, and every shoveled path now is deadly slick. I skate and scrabble my way once more to the barn and return with a sled Father built for Darrel when he was a boy. It's a bit small for him now, but he can fold himself up and sit on it, and I can stomp my way through the ice and pull him to school this way. He pretends to propel us along with his crutch as if the sled were a boat.

No signs of life at your house yet, and knowing Darrel's eyes are on me, I hide my looking.

We arrive at school early, which I intended. It gives me time to get Darrel unwrapped and into his seat before the other students arrive. Only the schoolmaster is there, feeding the fire.

"Well," he says, seeing us come in. "This is an unexpected pleasure. Miss Finch." He kisses my hand, which I hadn't offered. How dare he be so forward? "And Master Finch. So good to have you back in class. We'll have you caught up with your classmates in no time."

I stand aside while the schoolmaster bends over the books Darrel has brought with him, murmuring his approval and pointing with long white fingers to the pages they'll examine today. At length he turns and notices that I am still here.

"It was kind of you to help your brother get here," he says, brushing his hair back off his forehead. "Dismissal time is at three o'clock, if you'd like to return then to help him get home."

Darrel intervenes.

"She's not leaving. She's enrolling," he tells the school-master. "She wants to learn to read. She'll be staying with me here when I come."

Rupert Gillis stands up straighter and peers down at me with a gleam in his eye. "Well," he says. "This is an opportunity, isn't it?" He rubs his hands together. Students start to enter the schoolhouse, boys and girls bundled to their nostrils in winter wraps. They chatter together until they see Darrel and me.

"Let's see." The schoolmaster strides about the room. "Where shall we put you? With the others near your age? No, not the lads. You haven't had much schooling, have you? Can you read? I thought not." A pair of older girls in the back twitter.

The schoolroom fills rapidly now. Great boys swagger in and thump Darrel on the shoulder. I feel beads of sweat form on my forehead as all those eyes wonder at my presence. I hear little snorts of laughter. Reverend Frye's red-haired daughter, Elizabeth, slips in, sees me, and looks away. She's only two years younger than me, but it might be a dozen, she seems so young and shy.

The schoolmaster claps his hands, making me jump. "I have it." He pulls a chair up next to his own. "You shall sit here beside me, so that I can mentor you directly. That way you'll be spared the need to speak recitations with the part-ner at your desk. You won't have to sit with the very young children at your level, nor with the lads closer to your age." He rubs the seat of the chair beside him by way of inviting me to sit there.

My face is hot, yet I feel frozen. My skirts brush against

my legs as I walk to his desk. The rustling bounces off the schoolroom rafters.

"Good morning, students," Rupert Gillis says. "I'm sure we'll all want to welcome Master Darrel Finch back to school. And now we have a new student. I'm sorry." He smiles a closed-lip smile. "Master Finch, remind me of your sister's name?"

XVIII.

All morning I watch my hands, which lie folded in my lap. This doesn't protect me from seeing the eyes of the entire classroom riveted on me, despite Mr. Gillis leaping around the room, writing out arithmetic problems on each child's slate. When I hear them all scratching away at their work, I venture to look up. Several older girls and boys from the back row stare at me with unblinking, expressionless eyes. Here I sit by the teacher's desk, on display, as if I'm being punished.

To divert myself I look over Mr. Gillis's desk. There is little to see. A stack of primers, an ink pot and quill, a ruler, a book of maps. His possessions are as nondescript as his person.

And then, he slides into the chair beside me and favors me with a small smile.

"There now," he whispers, and leans toward me. "Shall we get started?"

Eyebrows rise throughout the classroom.

"The first step is to assess what you already know. This may prove challenging since you can't, er, tell me. But we'll figure it out as we go."

I feel mortified. This is scandalous, and the twenty

students watching him whisper to me know it. His breath blows sour in my face. My ambition to read grows shakier by the moment.

"There." He draws an *A* on his slate. His fingernails are stained with lead. "Do you know what that is?"

I nod my head. On the way to school that morning I'd considered revealing that I could speak. What better place than school? But the schoolmaster repulses me. I won't entrust my secret to him.

Somehow I endure the morning. He quizzes me on my letters and, with an extra slate, he sets me to work copying them out. After that, he gives me the most elementary primer and asks me to sound out the first lesson's words in my head. *It. At. If. Is. Up. On. As. An.*

I can already do this, and much more, but that is all right with me. I am content to start at the very beginning. Reading is worth learning in the proper way. I can be patient.

He dismisses the class for lunch, and the students get their pails. I'm grateful for the chance to leave my seat and sit by Darrel while we share our meal. He's uncomfortable, I can see. His wound still pains him. At home he'd lie down by this point in the day and take some rest.

While the others are busy with their food, I lean over and whisper in his ear, "We cahn go home. You can shleep. We cahn come back thomorrow." I lean back and watch Darrel's face. He looks torn and tempted.

"Want to?" he whispers.

I nod.

"Fetch Mr. Gillis?"

It isn't hard to convey to the schoolmaster that my brother

wishes to speak to him. He bends over and listens to Darrel, then nods his head.

"Certainly," I hear him murmur. "You must ease your way back until you're more able. Let's give you a reading assignment for this afternoon . . . there. These pages will do nicely."

I gather our coats and help Darrel into his. By this time the other students are getting their coats to go outside and walk about and throw snowballs, so our departure is not remarkable. Mr. Gillis holds the door open for us as I help Darrel descend the icy steps. He jumps down after us and helps situate Darrel in the sled.

"Good to have you back, Master Finch." He seizes my hand between both of his and fixes me with his gaze. "I'm honored," he says, "to have you as my newest pupil."

Out of sight to anyone watching, under the cover of his upper hand, he caresses a slow circle on my palm with a fingertip.

XIX.

The colonel did things like that. Run his hand down my arm. Stroke the sides of my neck with his thumb and forefinger, just under my jawbone. Trace his nail down the sole of my stockinged foot as I lay on my cot.

XX.

I can't pull Darrel home fast enough. Twice he complains of my jostling him. The sun is hard at work melting the snow, but last night's ice has proved impenetrable. Now the ice remains with a slick of water over its surface. I am stumbling and sliding with every other step, barely able to pull the sled without traction under my feet. Darrel takes a spill from the sled and gets wet and chilled all over. This will only be fat in Mother's fire.

How I dread going back tomorrow. I won't do it. I don't have to.

And that would be a whole pig's worth of fat in the fire.

I heave Darrel back onto the sled and set off once more.

XXI.

I thought if I could read and write, I could get my hands on some books and paper before I set out for the cabin in the spring. Then I could fill my days, whatever hours weren't spent surviving, on learning and thinking. I thought there could be solace in words.

Solace, I begin to think, is only a fantasy.

XXII.

Mother makes no mention of our having gone to school, but there is triumph in her eyes. She thinks we came home early because the school experiment failed. Neither Darrel nor I want to give her that victory. So, tired though he is, Darrel sits by the fire all afternoon and scrapes dried corn off the ears with his thumb, and picks through beans ready for soaking.

I sit opposite him and knit a pair of heavy stockings out of coarse gray wool. The steady flow of yarn through my fingers subdues me. I have already presented him, secretly, with his book bag. He was pleased. Now that Mother knows of our schooling plans, there seemed no more need to hide it.

"It was good to be back in class," Darrel announces loudly. "Doesn't appear I've fallen far behind."

Mother wrings wash water out of one of Darrel's shirts.

"Awfully good of Judith to take me," he goes on. "I'm in her debt. And what do you suppose? Mr. Gillis has her sitting right beside him so he can tutor her closely."

At this, Mother looks up at me.

"You see to it you're cordial to the schoolmaster." She wags the wet shirt at me.

I show no more emotion than my ball of yarn.

"He just may fancy you, God willing. So do as he tells you." She drowns another shirt in her bucket.

Darrel's mouth hangs open. "Mother, Gillis doesn't have designs on Judith."

"Much you'd know if he did," Mother says, elbow deep in suds. "She's got her own future to think of, and she'd best think wisely."

XXIII.

I lie in bed torn and unable to sleep. I dread sitting next to Rupert Gillis for even another hour. I dread my mother attempting to form a match for me.

But I also dread her exulting in our failure to return to school. And I dread disappointing Darrel, the great pest, in spite of everything he does to aggravate me.

One more day. I have endured worse than Rupert Gillis for years on end. I can endure one more day.

XXIV.

"How long have you been speaking, Judith?" Darrel asks me on the way into town the next morning.

I halt the sled and scowl at him. I silently rehearse the sounds I'll need in advance. Yes. "Before you were bornh," I say with all the aggravation I can muster.

Darrel laughs. "I know *that*. I mean, since. You know. All this time you say nothing, and now all of a sudden, you're talking. Why is that?"

I consider how to answer his question, or if I even want to. Is Maria the reason? Were you, at first? Off in my lonely cabin, with whom do I plan to speak?

"Shick of it," I finally say. "Ahways shtuck. People think I'm shtupidh. Or I'm noth there."

Darrel nods solemnly. "That's how they think about me, too."

I heave the sled along once more. No it isn't, you selfish baby. There's no comparison. Nobody thinks you're stupid. No one ever could. But empathy is dear in my world, so I'll take it.

We arrive at school just as the schoolmaster appears at the doorway to beckon the students inside. Not a moment sooner.

Darrel seems more at ease greeting his schoolmates today. A couple of them grab him under the arms and carry him in. He laughs and protests. He's no sooner through the door than a large, wet snowball plasters itself across my back. I do not turn to look. I hurry up the stairs, shake my coat off in the rear of the room, hang it, and sit at the schoolmaster's desk, taking care to move my chair as far from his as I can.

After calling the class to attention, Mr. Gillis spreads before me a large sheet of rough paper and hands me a lead pencil. "Copy these three times each," he says, opening a book to a page of letters. I am pleased; his manner is straightforward, almost brusque. Some tension slides off me. He is a schoolteacher, and he intends to teach. That is all. Very well, that is why I came.

I set to work copying the letters carefully. My fingers are nearly as clumsy as my mouth, but I write smaller and find room to copy each letter not three but five times. Midway through the alphabet, I can tell that I'm improving. Even at this beginner level, there's a thrill to grasping the smooth pencil between my finger and thumb, smelling the paper, blowing away the little flecks of gray dust that trail after the marks I've made. I envy the schoolmaster. Even as green as I am at this, I can easily see that I would rather spend my days with words than with chickens and mothers and brothers.

Rupert Gillis slides noiselessly into his chair. He peers over my work.

"You have exquisite hands." He is so quiet, not even the six-year-olds in front can hear.

The lead snaps off the tip of my pencil. He is not referring to my penmanship.

"Let me show you how to slant your letters." He envelops my hand in his and guides the pencil stump in forming a *T*. As soon as he pauses, I pull my hand away.

"Now you see how it goes," he says, and slides back to his regular place.

XXV.

Later in the morning, he sets the class to reading in pairs. Their murmurs make a timid if polite chorus that obscures his voice when he talks to me. This cover encourages him to talk more. I rather miss the silence.

I open the primer he loaned me yesterday and begin wallowing through the second lesson. I haven't gotten far when he places his long-fingered hand over the pages.

"Someone of your maturity must find these elementary primers dull," he says. "I wonder if you would be more interested in the classics? A bit of Roman poetry? I've made a particular study of it myself. Let me read to you."

Roman poetry, on my second day of school?

"Don't worry." He laughs softly. "It's not in Latin."

He opens the bottom drawer of his desk and removes a box. With a key from his vest pocket, he unlocks the box and pulls out a canvas-covered volume. *O, V, I, D*, I read on the front.

"These are tales of the pagan gods," he whispers with a glance toward the little ones in the front row. "They predate Christianity. Reverend Frye might not endorse them, but I find them quite diverting." He thumbs through the pages.

"Ah," he says. "Here's something you'll enjoy. It's the story of Io. She was forced by Jove, the king of the gods."

It takes me a second to comprehend his meaning of "forced." Rupert Gillis seems to find this amusing.

"Jove turned her into a lovely white cow," he said, "to hide his deed from Juno, his wife. Juno tormented Io, until finally Jove appeased Juno and she relented. Here we are."

And Juno, satisfied, gave Io back
The shape to which she had been born.
Rough, hairy cow's hide sloughed away
From off her body and her breast,
Leaving tender flesh behind.
Her horns shrank back into a head
More delicately sized, with eyes
And mouth of womanly proportion.
And where hooves and cattle legs had been,
Came graceful shoulders, round arms, hands—
Slender hands with fingers five, each tipped
With nails like polished gems.

Gillis bestows another meaningful glance upon my hands, and I hide them under the desk.

Gone, all trace of the cow she'd been,
Save the snowy whiteness of her skin.

I never heard a man speak so boldly, so rudely to a woman. I never knew words could act like fingers, touching where they ought not, grasping their pleasure at the victim's expense.

On two uncertain feet she stood
And feared her long unpracticed throat,
If tested, might, instead of speech,
Keep the mournful lowing she had known.
So hushed, and secretly she parted lips,

Gillis turns to look at me.

And trembling, spoke in her lost voice.

"So," he says, looking pleased with himself, "you and Io could understand each other, couldn't you? Yet you might say, if you could, that Io was the lucky one."

Because her voice came back.

Whatever pleasure Rupert Gillis intended to taste by exposing me to these words, I will not give up willingly. My face is flat, my soul elsewhere, my expression as numb as my feelings.

Not his. He puts away the Latin book and wipes the surface of his desk, as if crumbs of filth might have fallen from its pages. He folds his hands leisurely and surveys his pupils with a placid air of contentment.

Io was the lucky one. It is tempting to try my hand at some words a Christian young lady ought not to know. They are part of the colonel's legacy to me. But speech feels like intimacy now. Like a sacrament, a consummation. My words are not for Rupert Gillis. So instead I let my body speak.

I rise from my seat, gathering my slate and stylus, and move toward the third row of desks, where Eunice's twin younger sisters, a pair of plump, fair-haired girls of around twelve, have room enough to admit me to join their bench. They don't like me being there, but they say nothing.

I return the schoolmaster's gaze and see pink spots form on his cheeks. He digs for a kerchief in his jacket pocket and wipes his forehead, then rings the bell for dinner.

XXVI.

He submits the class in the afternoon to oral spelling, arithmetic, and grammar examinations with cold-blooded determination. He even quizzes me, and when I won't answer,
he brings his ruler down on my outstretched hand. Three
times he summons me to the front of the room, demanding
that I spell "funerary" and "pristine" and "obsidian." I say
nothing and take his strokes, then return to my seat where
the blonde girls regard me with either admiration or terror.
Elizabeth Frye doesn't dare meet my eye.

I listen as the other students recite their answers. A few
make mistakes and receive strokes, but not, I think, as fierce as
mine. Darrel answers all his questions quickly and well, and
in spite of my stinging hand, or perhaps because of it, I am
proud of my clever brother.

His wrath appeased, the schoolmaster finishes the afternoon's lessons, skipping me entirely when he makes his
rounds. I watch clumps of soft snow fall from branches outside the window until it's time to leave. They are white, and
soft, and lovely. Like Io, when she was a cow.

I think of myself transforming—the horns that aren't
there, that everyone sees, receding into my head.

But I am no cow, and there is no goddess to forgive me for
what I never did.

XXVII.

You pass by the window. I turn to see. Is that, in fact, you?
It's you, and you see me now. The schoolmaster half rises
from his seat.

He rings the dismissal bell and reaches the door before the students can grasp their freedom and get there first.

"Whiting." His voice is hearty and convivial. As if you and he are longtime friends. "Good to see you. What brings you here?"

"I've come to help the Finches home." Your voice reaches me through the press of students jostling for their coats.

His delay betrays him, but only to me. "Good man," he says. "Right neighborly. Judith! Darrel!" Not Master and Miss this time. He turns and catches me with a gleaming eye. "Your royal escort awaits." The girls titter, the boys scoff, and the schoolmaster returns, satisfied, to his seat.

XXVIII.

You lean against a tree, with Jip romping around your heels. Good old Jip.

"Good afternoon, er, Miss Finch," you say, and extend me a hand, then seem to hesitate, as if embarrassed. I seize your hand and shake it.

Darrel's comrades, two tall boys, drag him out, his good leg and his bad one dangling over the snow. They deposit him on his sled and clap you on the back, eager to show they're nearly men now themselves. Which one of them plastered me with snow this morning, I wonder.

"I thought you could use a hand with the sled this afternoon." You take hold of the rope and start out over the muck. "This thaw makes the going rough."

"Thank you," I say, nearly as well as anyone else might.

"Tomorrow, why don't I pull you in the mule cart?" you say. "This mud will only get worse."

"You *are* a royal escort," Darrel calls out. "Driven to school in the mule cart! Hurrah!"

You glance at me, and we both smile.

The school is far behind us now, and the air feels freer to me already. Only when my shoulder aches begin to fade do I realize how much the day's worry has tied up my flesh into tangled knots.

"Say, Lucas," Darrel calls out, "you wouldn't believe how Gillis treated Judith today. Something awful."

You stop pulling the sled, and Darrel flops forward.

"Watch it!" he calls. I look to see if his fall affected his stump.

"You all right, Darrel?" you ask. When he says yes, you turn to me.

"What did he do to you?"

I try to remain nonchalant. Are you angry? Not at me, surely?

I speak slowly, which gives me time to form the sounds as near as I can. "He didn't care for how litthle I know."

Darrel can't bear this. He waves wildly to get your attention. "He sat her in the front of the class, right at his desk, so he could tutor her specially. Whispered in her ear all day, more like. But he must have said something cruel, because she up and left his desk in the morning and sat with the fifth-level girls. Did he ever get vexed! So then in the afternoon he made everyone do double recitations and examinations, and he punished her for saying nothing! Gave her fifth-level words to spell, too."

Your fingers flex inside your gloves. "What did he say that upset you?"

Darrel! I glare at my brother. Why did you do this to me?

"I can't sshay," is my answer. The words come out limp and pathetic, as they are.

"Won't say, you mean." Your voice is bitter.

You set off again with a heave at the rope on Darrel's sled. I'm glad to be moving. But what have I done wrong?

"Show him your hand, Judith," Darrel calls.

You stop once more, and I know you won't be appeased until you've seen my palm. I peel off my mitten and hand it to you. There's a raised welt where he struck me. On the third stroke it bled.

You take my hand carefully and examine the stripe. "I should report this to the aldermen."

"Dhon't," I say. "They care for me lesh than for you, now."

And that, I can see, was both foolish and mean. You deposit the sled at the door of the house and retreat after the briefest of good-byes.

Maria has taught me anew how to speak; I must teach myself better, when not to.

XXIX.

Darrel sits up after Mother has gone to bed, listening to me read through my primer that night. The words are easy to read: *cat, rat, sat, sit, bat, bit, fat.* They're less easy for me to say. *Catth. Ratth. Satth.* My thick stump of a tongue can't make the delicate sound of a single *T.* That requires the flick of a narrow tip. Whatever I do, a *th* tail lingers behind.

"Try them again, Judy," Darrel says. He's caught Maria's

fever, and forgotten that his job is to be my reading tutor, not my elocution mistress.

"Sitth. Batth. Bitth."

"Cut it off shorter," he says. "You're almost there."

"Catt. Ratt. Satt."

He's right. It is sounding better. The *H* is fading. But it will never sound right. Thrusting my tongue so far forward to compensate for what it has lost makes me sound mentally weak.

There was a big lad in the village when I was young whose mind wasn't fully right. Nor was his speech. He didn't live long. He drowned in the river when the spring floods were high. I hear his odd voice in my attempts, and I close the primer.

XXX.

A warm wind blows through the night and I lie awake in bed listening to icicles melt and drip off the eaves.

I think of returning to school. I'd rather disappear. Or better, strangle Rupert Gillis.

No. I should never jest like that, not even to myself.

I saw Lottie strangled. Her life was snuffed out like the wick of a lamp. Even foul Rupert Gillis deserves his fetid breath.

But how can I let his Latin poems and his stinging ruler prevail? I want to learn. I deserve to read and write. Thoughts for company, and a pen for a voice. Who is more entitled to those privileges than I?

XXXI.

I saw life choked out, squeezed out of my young friend. Saw the lights in her eyes extinguished by a pair of hands, hands so filthy they soiled the triangle lace of her dress collar.

To think of dirty collars at such a time.

Whose hands they were, I couldn't see.

I watched her lose her breath forever while I sat in the willow tree holding mine, lest he find me, too, and his hands press into my soft neck like dirty boots into new-fallen snow.

XXXII.

Morning comes, and nearly all the snow is gone. There is no need for you to drive us to school in the mule cart. But you come. Darrel sits in back on a hay bale, and Jip twists in happy circles at his feet. I go to sit next to him, but you insist I sit beside you. A courteous gesture.

I fix my eyes on your mule's rump and smell the wood-smoke scent that rises off your brown wool coat.

You chuck the reins and we set off.

"Ugly, isn't she?"

I look up. You mean the mule.

I protest this. My speech is slow and careful. "Nott for whatt she is."

You grin. "Where'd you get your speckled mare?"

I wait for Darrel to answer but he doesn't. I turn to see him; he's watching the passing scenery with a determination that I don't trust for an instant. But it appears I must speak. I choose my words carefully.

"At the battle. Her owner was killed."

"Oh?"

Phantom could have been one of the soldiers' from Pinkerton, but I imagine you know she wasn't.

"I call her Phanttom." My conscience compels me to add, in a lower voice, "She should be yours."

"Get along! Git!" you shout to your mule, who has found a patch of greens unearthed by the snow.

You settle back into your seat. "Phantom. Where'd you come up with that name?"

"She's more ghostht than animal."

Your eyes invite me to keep talking.

"Shometimes I think she reads my thoughts."

You laugh a little. "*My* thoughts would make dull reading. Git along, you dumb mule!"

Then I start to laugh.

"What's so funny?"

"*Dhumb* mule." I tap my breastbone.

Your face flushes. I try to suppress my laughter.

"Well, you're not!" you say.

I'm surprised at your vehemence. "Mostt people think I am."

"Hmp."

You turn back to the road, even though your mule could drive us to town blindfolded. I go back to watching her swaying rump and trying not to laugh.

"Why have you waited so long to speak?"

It is Darrel's question all over again, and still I'm unprepared for it. No one wanted to hear what I had to say. I didn't think I could. Mother wouldn't let me. I didn't want to. I don't know. I was waiting for Maria to decide I could. None of your affair.

I sit up a little taller in my seat. "Now is better than later."

You watch me, then turn away, but not before I catch you grin. You tip your hat to me, like one who admits he's been bested in a friendly duel. "And so it is, Ladybird."

I turn in astonishment, but your gaze is fixed upon the road.

XXXIII.

We pass the first houses of town. When you speak again, it startles me.

"So, a horse that can read your thoughts. Wonder what she sees."

I speak without thinking. "You do?"

"I figure you do some of the better thinking that goes on in this town."

Ah. Men in Roswell Station, men everywhere for that matter, don't usually consider it a virtue for a woman to be adept at thinking. But I wonder. I think about my father. I believe he was proud of Mother's strong will and quick wit. Perhaps I judge too quickly.

"Mother isn't happy about Phanttom," I say.

"Oh?"

"Too much for feed."

"Hm."

We pull up in front of the schoolhouse. I see Rupert Gillis's face peering out through a smeared windowpane. Darrel is grabbed bodily by two of his friends and hauled into school, leaving Jip yapping.

"You could stable Phantom at my house," you say.

I feel conscience pressing in on me. I should have given her to you at the start.

"She should be yours," I repeat.

"No," you say, "she's yours. But I can board her for you. And you can come visit her as often as you like."

Before I can comprehend your words, I'm nodding and accepting the offer. If you take her, I don't really lose her, and I never want to say good-bye to Phantom.

Jip squirms into the front of the cart and licks your face. You shoo him off and help me down from the cart.

"Don't be upset, though," you say, "if I ask Phantom to tell me what she sees when she reads your mind."

XXXIV.

Rupert Gillis shows no reaction when I sit down in my seat with the fifth-grade girls. Throughout the morning he operates as if all is normal. He comes to my seat, corrects my work, and assigns me new exercises and words to copy. He gives me nothing beyond my grasp. He instructs indifferently and moves on to the next pupil.

I begin to think I've prevailed. Perhaps yesterday was nothing more than a juvenile attempt he'll abandon. We can move forward as teacher and student, and I can learn to read. Already my writing is improving, and I've read several lessons ahead in my primer.

At lunchtime he dismisses the class, but calls me to his desk. I prepare myself to be silent in both face and body.

"I had some visitors yesterday, Miss Finch. Interestingly enough, they all came to see me concerning you." He waits for me to respond, then continues. "The first ones were Mr. and Mrs. Robinson, whose girls sit by you. Mrs. Robinson objects to your presence in the school. She claims you are an immoral influence on her girls. Her husband shares her concern."

Robinson. Eunice's younger sisters. I pretend to cough.

"It left me in an awkward position. Naturally I tried to reassure them both. Frankly, I don't see what's immoral about you sitting in class. But I was hard-pressed to counter their charges concerning your virtue."

He's startled me despite my defenses.

He nods at my changed expression.

"The other visitor was a friend and protector of yours, it seems. He used language ill fitting a gentleman to urge me to treat you fairly in my classroom."

My insides squirm. Did you do that? Confront the schoolmaster on my behalf?

Perhaps some child took home a report of my ill treatment, and his father spoke on my behalf out of Christian decency.

But I don't think so.

"Some for you, some against you. A woman of controversy." The schoolmaster pushes back his chair and stands. "Your mind is not inferior, Judith." He comes around the corner of his desk. "You're sadly behind for your age, but you could learn much if you had closer instruction."

He stands so close, he is peering down the length of his nose at me.

"I could help you. I could tutor you at length this evening, at my home, if you came to me."

There is no mistaking the gleam in his spectacled fish's eyes.

I back away but he seizes my wrist. His grip is surprising for one so thin. I shake my head violently and try to pry his hand away with my other.

"A maidenly display," he says. "But we both know differently." I can smell his heat through his musty woolens. "There is no use pretending you don't know what I need, when I've seen you come from Lucas Whiting's cabin, scarcely dressed, in the middle of the night."

No. Oh no no no.

He knows he hit a mark that time. Again he traces circles on my captive palm with his free finger.

"If him, then why not me? I like a girl who doesn't tell tales."

I struggle to free my hand. Then I stomp my foot on his toes. He lets me go, utterly at ease. There is a sound of stamping boots at the door. We both look to see one of Darrel's friends come indoors. I feel smeared in grease, so polluting are the schoolmaster's words and eyes upon me.

"If not, then we'll let Mrs. Robinson and the town decide if you deserve to be taught. Yes, Master Pawling? What can I do for you?"

XXXV.

When you come to drive us home from school in the mule cart, Darrel and I are bundled and ready, but we must wait while Rupert Gillis flaunts his pretended friendship with you.

"So good of you to look after these poor unfortunates," he says to you. "You're a model of Christian charity toward them." Your face darkens.

You say nothing at all on the whole ride home. Nor do you so much as look at me.

Can Gillis have said something to you about seeing me leave your house?

XXXVI.

The sudden cold and rapid thaw are no helpers to the squashes. I visit the heap in the barn, pick out the two pumpkins most affected, and heave them onto a butchering block. One is round and fat and wrinkly, the other tall and smooth and skinny. The latter is clearly Rupert; the former, I decide, is Goody Pruett. I chop Goody Pruett into chunks, scoop her pulp, and peel her skin with Mother's butchering knife. The tang of pumpkin fills my nostrils. Person's, too. She lows for some.

Then I take the hatchet to Rupert and scalp him, leaving a lovely hole. I scoop out his pulpy brains and seeds and dump them in a pail for Person. Indoors on the hearth, a pan of water heats, ready to simmer the pumpkin until it's soft.

The door to the barn opens and I look up, expecting to see Mother.

It's you, silhouetted in the doorway of the barn in late afternoon light.

Despite the late season you're clad only in a shirt and pants. No hat or coat. I am elbow deep in pumpkin mess, wearing a soiled apron that I quickly remove and lay aside.

"What are you making?" You come farther inside and reach out a hand to stroke Phantom's neck.

I scrub at my syrupy arm with my apron. "Ssttew."

Your fingertips make Phantom nicker with pleasure.

"Sounds good."

"Where's Jip?"

You grin. "Locked him home, the mongrel. He stole my dinner today when my back was turned."

I'm slow with my manners. You haven't had dinner. "Would you sstay and have ssome?"

"Some what?"

Oh dear. My face must be red. "Pumpkin. Ssttew."

You reach for the knife and start shaving the skins off the chunks. "I don't know how well your mother would enjoy that."

I can't pretend you're mistaken.

"I would like to, though." You reach for another pumpkin piece. "Why does your mother dislike me?"

I set down my hatchet and look at you. How can I answer this? I can't.

"I could ask the same quesstion," I say. "I think, after I . . . went away, and Father died, all the love she had left wentt to Darrel."

You're watching me closely. My answer doesn't satisfy you. "But you came back!"

I shook my head. "Not the ssame. Not for her."

You set down your knife and lean against the wall with your arms folded across your chest. "That must hurt."

This conversation has taken much too sad a turn. Time for a change. I point to the scalped pumpkin. "This is Mr. Gilliss." I split him in two with my hatchet.

The juicy *crack* of the cleaving pumpkin makes you jump. You smile and reach for the hatchet. "Let me have a go at Gillis." Soon the schoolteacher's head lies in small pieces on the block. You reach for the pumpkin chunk you were peeling before. "This one isn't me, I hope."

"Oh, it is."

"I thought as much."

Your smile fades. "Is Gillis still troubling you?"

I consider what to say. I don't want you to think me weak if I admit that he is.

You seem to accept my unwillingness to answer. You go to Phantom's stall and stroke her neck. "I came to talk with you about something."

Your somber tone worries me. "Phanttom?"

"No." You run your hands through her mane. "But I'm glad to take her in whenever you decide."

I'm relieved that you don't claim her. But then why have you come, if not for my horse? I drop my hatchet and take a pumpkin chunk over to her stall. She devours it and noses my sticky hands for more. I press my cheek against the hard bone of her face. What do you say, girl? Will you be happy if you go live with Lucas?

Phantom nibbles my cheek in answer and nudges against me as if to shove my reluctance away. And then we're both there, side by side, stroking her dappled hide. You take up a brush and groom her in earnest, so I pick up a comb and start working on her mane.

The barn grows rapidly darker now. Only bits of reddish gold filter through gaps in the beams. I sense, more than see, you standing beside me.

"She'll be happy with you," I tell you. "Take her today. Mother will be gladh." I put on a brave smile, but my heart aches at the thought of coming to the barn each morning and finding Phantom gone.

You are so close beside me that we almost touch each other as we groom my horse.

I stiffen and wait for you to move aside.

And then you're behind me, brushing against me while one arm reaches around me to curry Phantom with slow, fluid strokes.

What is happening?

You stop, drop the brush, and lean against me. You rest your jaw in my bonnet and wrap your fingers around my arms.

I'm so confused I panic. I don't want to be touched.

"No," I say.

Immediately you step back and look away. You stand there looking mortified, and then you make as if to leave. You are at the door.

"Why?" I say.

You stop. "Why what?"

I am trying to breathe, and trying not to cry. I can barely comprehend what has just happened, but I need to know why. I once would have given anything for a touch from you. Your father may have taken away my girlhood, but it's Rupert Gillis who has opened my eyes. I'll not be the pet of men who feel like touching something, anything. I'll not be thought easy to have for having been had before.

I hate to think it of you. If we ever were friends, neighbors, children together, let me believe you would not use me cruelly, nor even for your selfish comfort.

So I demand to know your reason why.

"Why me?" I take another breath. "Why this?"

I force you to look at me from across the barn. I will not let your eyes escape mine.

There is only the sound of Phantom breathing and Person chewing.

"It was always you, Ladybird," you say softly. "Don't you know?"

XXXVII.

Nothing can restrain my tears from falling now.

You hate to see them, and you take a step toward me, reaching out your hand.

I wipe my eyes fiercely on my loose apron.

"Then what about Maria?"

You nod. You can't deny my asking.

"I'm sorry about Maria," you say. "Not sorry that it ended. Not now." Your eyes plead with me. "Forgive me, Judith."

Forgive you? "For what?"

You make no sense. Who can blame you for courting Maria? Who can blame anyone for succumbing to her appeal?

"Maria is wonderful," I say. "She is very beautiful, and kindh."

Your smile is sad. "Leon is a lucky man."

I will not be satisfied with merely this as your answer. How can you say it was always me? You have more explaining to do.

You swallow and plow on. "Maria deserves every happiness. But I never had her heart, and I see now, she never had mine."

I am trying to understand, I am trying to think, trying to feel, trying to forgive, trying to stay standing on my own two feet.

"I was unfair to her, and untrue to myself." You rake your fingers through your hair. "Judith, since we were little, I've been waiting for the day when I could tell you this."

What can be happening here? Can you truly have come a-wooing tonight when you entered my barn?

I lean against Phantom's stall and wrap my arms around a post. How many times had I dreamed that you might one day feel for me one fragment of what I've felt for you? But what you have not yet said is still larger and more final than all you have.

"And my ttongue? My sspeech?"

Still you do not look away from me. I am waiting for even the smallest twitch. Instead, you take one step closer, though a gulf still stands between us, and I will not let you bridge it.

You cannot pass this test and be truthful. What shall you say? That it doesn't matter to you at all how I sound? That whole or marred makes no difference to you? For clearly, it made a difference before, when you chose to go a-calling at Maria's door.

"It's a cruel world," you say. "Why did it have to happen? And to you?"

Phantom nudges my back with her nose. These are questions I can't answer.

Your eyes grow wet. "I let it get in the way."

I nod and look away. I can breathe again It's done.

Thank you for being honest with me.

It's good of you to say all this. What you've given me

tonight will help me to heal. I see that I can forgive you for all of it, now. For affection running cold, for moving past me and falling under Maria's spell. For wondering about your father and wounding me with probing questions. You're only human, as am I.

You're a good man, Lucas. A kind and decent man. Some misfortunes ruin our hopes. And that is all. We might even have grown up and married and been happy together, my little-girl dreams and even your growing-boy dreams coming true, but tragedy intervened. We are not the first for whom it has.

Tonight, I think, you mistook pity and remorse for desire. Loneliness made you confused. Heaven knows I have long been confused about you, too.

I truly forgive you, Lucas. And I will always wish you well.

I feel my sadness float away, my regret and humiliation. I can forgive myself for the fool I've made myself before you. The awkwardness is over. My body is left empty, and empty is a great relief.

XXXVIII.

I hold out my hand to you, for peace, and for friendship. "Thank you," I say. "You've been kindh. You can go. Mother will come looking ssoon."

You take my hand, but you look bewildered. "I'm not done," you say. "I came because—"

"Ssome other time," I say. We both hear the banging of the door to my house. I point to the rear door of the barn. "Quick, that way, through the woods, or Mother will see you."

I push you toward the door, but you protest all the way.

"Judith, please, there's something I need to tell you."

"Go!" I hiss. "Later!"

At the last second you disobey completely. Instead of leaving, you vault over the top of Person's stall. The squelching sound and the stink would tell me what you've landed in, even if your groaning laughter didn't.

In spite of myself I start laughing, too.

Mother enters the barn, and we both make ourselves still.

"So you've got my knife."

"Umm-hm."

She sniffs. "Ugh! Haven't you cleaned out the stalls today?"

I mustn't laugh. "Unh-uh," I lie. I can't let her inspect them.

"Can't hardly see a thing in this dark. What's taking you so long out here? Your pot's been boiling a while now."

I know she doesn't really want me to answer, which is just as well.

"We can't keep that mare, you know," she says, revisiting a favorite theme. "Suppose that Whiting boy's got enough to buy it off us?"

"Mmmm." I roll the note to say, I don't know.

"If he could afford Maria Johnson, he could afford a horse. I'll ask him next time I see him. Hurry and bring those squashes. Your brother's ready to eat the tablecloth."

I think of you crouching in cow dung and hearing this, and don't know whether to laugh or groan.

Mother goes back toward the house.

"You can come outt," I whisper.

You stand up, grinning broadly. "So I can afford Phantom, can I?"

"I don't know," I say. I am in a wicked mood. "Could you affordh Maria Johnson?"

You make a wry face, and I laugh.

"Good night, Lucass," I say. "Ssee you tomorrow."

You will not easily surrender the last word, but at last, you leave.

"Lucass?" I call after you.

You turn back.

"Wipe your feett."

I carry my pail of pumpkin chunks inside to fix for supper.

XXXIX.

Mother sends me back to the barn for the knife I forgot.

I feel curiously afloat tonight, like an autumn seed carried aloft on the air. Something holding me has released me, leaving me free to move.

I hug Phantom and kiss her nose, then Person, too, so she's not slighted. She deserves a better name than Person.

Io, of course. The beautiful cow.

I grab the knife and go back toward the house. I know the way with my eyes shut. I inhale the wild, warm autumn wind, smelling damp, dead leaves and soil and rotting apples and wood smoke carried on the breeze.

A twig cracks.

I stop and listen.

There is another step. It must be you, come back to tell me what you couldn't before. I wait for another step, and there it is. You're carrying a lantern, mostly shaded, with only slivers of light peeking through the slats.

The lantern approaches. Its light gleams on the edge of my knife.

It isn't you. He's not tall enough.

And now he, whoever he is, may be too close for me to run away.

I clutch the knife handle and brandish the blade before me.

It can't be the schoolmaster. He has your height and then some. This man is lower to the ground.

"Whatt do you wantt?" I call in the most menacing, fearless voice I can make.

The lantern stills. The footsteps stop. I hear a sound, like a grunt or an intake of breath, not enough for me to recognize a voice. I hear the grating sound of metal on metal, then the lantern closes completely. The man in the darkness begins to move.

I fly toward the house, leaping over tree roots that cross the path. My pursuer grunts again as he stumbles over them. I reach the safety of the door and the lamplight pouring from the windows. I wrench the door open and tumble in, slamming and bolting it behind me. Mother rises, wide-eyed, and runs to me while I pull down Father's flintlock from a high shelf. She takes the knife from my hand, and Darrel, to my surprise, pulls Father's pistol out from under his mattress.

"Bear?" Mother asks.

I try to calm my heaving breath, and shake my head. "Manh."

Mother's knuckles tighten around her knife. "Who?"

I shake my head. "I don't know."

Mother presses her face against the window, scanning the darkness for some trace.

"You sure you saw someone?" she asks after a time.

I nod decisively.

"We need to get a dog," Darrel says. I turn to look back at him, realizing I'd all but forgotten about him. He grips his crutch with one hand and dangles Father's pistol from the other.

"Put that away," Mother tells him, indicating the pistol. "We can't afford you losing both your feet."

Darrel's face flushes with shame but he says nothing. I feel sorry for him, but I confess, the same thought went through my own head.

XL.

All through dinner I pick at my food. Who is after me? It couldn't be Rupert Gillis. Mr. Robinson? Surely not. He is a shorter man, but he couldn't be. One of the louts from school?

Whoever it is, he's a coward. But a dangerous one. I hope he saw my knife.

I make up my mind to tell you about him next time I see you.

I think of our talk in the barn. All those years, and I was the girl on your mind? I suppose it's best that I never knew. Only a few days ago, any sign from you would have melted me. I have surprised myself tonight.

I think of your parting words. What was it you wanted to tell me?

XLI.

The next morning I wake well before dawn. I dress, and go out to tend to Phantom, Io, and the chickens. Io moos at me. She's still asleep and not ready for my attentions yet.

So instead I take the pail to the stream and dip it into the dark water to refill their trough. I have only turned back toward the house when I hear Jip bark and look up to see your shadow approaching through the predawn dark.

I set my bucket down.

"It's only me, Judith," you call out softly.

"I know."

You stand before me, and I wait for you to tell me why you've come. I know I have been wise to pull my heart back from you, but when you stand so close to me, you do not make it easy.

"You're up early," I say, to make conversation.

You remove your hat and crush the brim in both hands. "I hoped I'd find you. I needed to tell you something."

I wait and watch. The palest light begins to appear in the eastern sky. You have trouble starting. You seem torn by indecision.

"A group of men from the village are organizing an expedition," you say at last. "They'll leave in a few days to go find my father's 'lair.'" Your voice is bitter. "They hope to find the rest of the arsenal, and . . ." Your eyes have closed. ". . . and evidence that he was responsible for your captivity and Lottie Pratt's death."

I leave my bucket where it sits and begin to walk. I don't know what else to do. You turn and follow. My skirts swish through tall, dry grass.

"I wanted to warn you," you say. "Who knows if they'll find his home, or what they'll find if they do?"

His home. If they find his cabin, they'll take it from me. They may destroy it. But whether they do or not, it will no longer be a hidden sanctuary. As for what they might find, I can't think of anything besides some pans, utensils, and clothes, and whatever remains of the arsenal's stores.

I press on toward the woods.

Without my cabin to flee to in the spring, what remains for me?

The rising sun gives enough light for me to find my singing rock in the clearing. I sit down upon it. It is bitterly cold against my legs.

So I will live out my days with my mother and Darrel. There is nowhere else I can go. We three belong together. Our lives have left each of us ruined for anyone else.

You stand and watch my face with concern written across yours.

I comprehend your worry, besides my own. "Don't worry," I say. "There's nothing there that would accuse him."

And now I have told you.

You nod your head and press your lips together. Yes. Now you know. But you already did.

XLII.

You sit down beside me on the rock. It is so very cold on us both. We huddle together, our arms pressing against each other, for some bit of warmth.

"I volunteered to join them," you say, "but they refused me. They think I'd steer them astray. As if I knew where my father was all this time! If I had, I'd have . . ."

Gone to him? Tried to persuade him to come back home?

Your face is so close to mine that my eyes can't focus on all of you, only your moving lips.

"I tried to find him. Lord knows I did, dozens of times."

This is a new thought for me. I picture you, the lean youth as I remember you then, searching the forest for your father. "After he disappearedh?"

"No. After *you* disappeared."

It makes no sense. I look up in confusion. I can feel the warmth of your breath reaching through this frigid wind.

"When he went away, I believed he was dead. When Lottie disappeared, I began to wonder. When you did, I began to search."

I think of the nights I dreamed of you rescuing me, and I wonder how close you came. Near misses are our lot.

My teeth start to chatter. You shift your weight, and before I realize what is happening, I am tucked in closer to your side, and your arm is now wrapped behind me. Your cheek rests on the crown of my head.

I should object, but you are warm. And we have known each other for a long time.

"Forgive me, Judith." I can feel your words more than hear them. "I've been a fool."

My cap slides backward off my head. You pull it away and toss it onto your own abandoned hat. You take my face in both your hands, cradling my head and gazing into my eyes. I look for doubt in you, and find none. Nor do I find protest within me.

You rest your forehead against mine. Then you kiss the

crown of my head. Your mouth is buried inside my hair.

"Give me one more try," I hear you say. "Let me hear your voice, Ladybird. Always."

Tears fill my eyes and begin to drip into my lap. I am a child, digging you worms, watching you fish. I am a girl on the verge of growing up, dreaming of holding your hand. I am a young lady, taken away and maimed in more than my mouth. I am a grown young woman, cursed and cast aside, watching you walk beyond my reach forever.

And now I am here, past the end of hope, on a cold rock hearing you tell me—what is it that you are trying to tell me?

Through my tears you have gathered me into your arms and onto your lap. You are wrapped around me, pressed against me, once again, in these woods, this time awake. The weight of your arms around me could almost be enough for me.

What were all those years? Were they wasted desire?

I must say this. "I have loved you too long, Lucass."

You kiss my cheek, my temple, my chin.

"Too long?" you say. "No such thing."

I pull back and look at you. "What?"

"No such thing as too long," you say. You're smiling into my face, looking into my eyes. I don't know when I've ever seen you this happy. Not since you were very young.

"It's new as morning, for me, waking up to find I've been loving you for years."

I want to protest impossibility; I can't let myself believe you. But I can. A certainty envelops me. I *can* believe you.

But that doesn't mean I can't exact a price from you. I struggle to disentangle myself from your embrace and give you a stern look. "You have a fine way of sthowing it."

You laugh and tighten your hold.

"Did you know I used to watch you sing on this very rock with your father?" you say. "You must have seen me."

I sit up taller. "Never!"

You point to a large elm some distance away. "I'd hide over there and listen. I'll bet I spied on you dozens of times."

I look at the tree and wonder at it. How could I never have seen? I shake my head. "Oddh of you."

You raise your eyebrows. I smile. Yes, I am a fine one to call you odd for spying.

"Can you love me just a little longer, Judith?" you ask. "Long enough for me to speak to your mother?"

The thought of Mother startles me back into my skin, in the cold morning air.

"May I ask her permission to call on you?"

To call on me. I picture us sitting stiffly at Mother's table, and laugh out loud.

I pull away again to see your face. There, once more, I see your promise enfolding me, your offered heart, so longed for, and so new. Is this what love looks like? And do you really want to come courting me? This is real, and I know it, so why *now* do I cry?

"She won't believe you."

You smile. "Leave that to me."

You're laughing. You're covering me with kisses. Your arms are crushing me close to you. My tears drip all over your jacket. You stand up and twirl me around in a circle until I order you to put me down.

The sun is up now, and the autumn woods are bright with

eastern light on melting frost. Morning shadows of skeletal tree limbs stretch across your face.

You take both my hands in yours. "My father took you away from me once. I will never let him do it again."

It's terribly cold, even in the sunlight. My nose is turning numb. I reach for you and pull your head close to mine. I kiss your mouth. I feel your intake of breath as you receive my kiss, and return it.

I feel no more cold. Only this. Only you.

When it ends, I bury my face in your neck, and feel your arms wrap tighter around me. How can I let go?

"Don't worry about the menh," I whisper into your ear. "I doubt they'll find your father's cabin. If they do, there's nothing there to harm you."

You're not as convinced.

"Tell me how to find it, so I can go first and make sure?"

There seems little harm in that. "Phanttom could take you," I say. "She knows the trail." I describe the path and the blind crevice that leads to the colonel's valley.

"I'll go today," you say. "After I take you to school. Don't tell anyone."

It is your turn to kiss me now, and this time, I don't need to hide afterward. You smile.

"Look after Jip for me? I'll tie him in the barn."

XLIII.

Somehow you leave me and head for home, so that you can arrive later in the morning with your mule cart, just as I'm leading Phantom out of the barn on a rope. We can take her to your stable on our way to school.

It is impossible to be calm and pretend this morning never happened. Only years of being mute keep me from saying something stupid.

Jip squirms on the seat board beside you, flicking his tail in your face. Darrel climbs into the back. You jump down from the cart and tether Phantom to the back of it, then climb in and off we go. In no time, we're at your home. I wait in the cart while you lead Phantom into your barn.

"Phanttom will be happy, I think," I tell Darrel as if he'd been worried.

"If you say so," Darrel says with a shrug.

You climb back into the cart with a spring that sets it bouncing, and we set off. For the rest of the ride to town, you and Darrel keep up a running conversation about school, the weather, the season's hunting. I wonder if Darrel suspects anything. I wave in passing to Goody Pruett, whom we overtake on our way to town. She declines your offer of a ride. "Goody Pruett still has legs that can carry her, thank you kindly."

Saints preserve us from her prying eyes! What does she know? Nothing would surprise me from Goody.

I wish you weren't leaving today.

You must have read my thoughts, for you say, "I'm sorry I won't be able to pick you up after school today."

"No matter," I say. "Roads are clear enough."

In the center of town, alongside the square where the school and church stand, an assembly of men stands. Reverend Frye, dressed in clerical garb, stands atop the platform, addressing them.

They turn like a wall of accusing eyes to watch us as we come. Me, the mute girl who was taken and returned, and you, the son of the dragon. Together in a cart. Suspicion is written plainly on Abijah Pratt's whiskered face. I look to you and see your mouth set in a hard line, a vein throbbing in your neck.

XLIV.

An unendurable school morning, and not, this time, because of anything Rupert Gillis does. The blonde Robinson girls sitting beside me are taking lessons in kindness from their mother. I slip into my seat and hear a squelch, and smell something like cider. They've found an oozing, rotten apple and brought it to share with me. I feel the wetness soak through the seat of my skirt. For the rest of the day I smell foul, and the other students don't hide their laughter.

Never mind, I tell myself. I am used to this. I can bear it. I can bear anything today. Their cruelty can't touch me. Besides, I am well into the fourth section of my primer. Darrel is back at the head of his class after less than a week of lessons. These are the reasons we come.

I realize that I never told you about the man outside my house. No matter, I think. I'll tell you when you return tonight.

At the end of the day, the schoolmaster calls all the fifth-level students to the front of the room to be tested on their spelling words. This time I have memorized the spellings, so I bring my slate with me to write my words down and show that I know them. But he orders me to put my slate back. When I won't spell *harridan* aloud, Rupert Gillis brings his ruler whistling down repeatedly upon my hand, and says, before the whole class, "I've told you before that if you wish to remain a student in my class, you must come to me for extra tutoring to catch up. I can't leave you here to drag the rest of your class down. Come for tutoring this evening, or I shall be forced to speak to your mother."

Now he propositions me publicly.

XLV.

After school I take Darrel's elbow and lead him toward the street. I can't bear Rupert Gillis leering at us out the window and enjoying our abandonment. A walk this long will be hard on Darrel. It will surely aggravate the bruises that his crutch has already stamped on his tender armpit. But we have to get home, and perhaps this will toughen him.

We stop to rest many times along the way. When we arrive home from school, Darrel heaves himself into a chair and massages his underarm.

Goody Pruett is there, sharing a cup of bark coffee with Mother.

"Come to meeting, Eliza," she tells my mother. "If your boy is well enough to go t'school, he's well enough to come to meeting, and you alongside him. Goody Pruett's warning you, they'll slap a sentence on you if you don't. Goody's got ears. She hears what goes around."

Mother's face is grim, but she nods her head. The last thing she needs is an hour in the pillory for failing to go to church. She doesn't need any more public humiliation than I've already caused her.

I head outdoors to the barn to say hello to Person. That

is, Io. I imagine she misses Phantom, but in truth I'm the one who's bereft. On my way, I think of Darrel's words to me on the slow walk home.

"Why are you still coming to school, Judy?"

I didn't answer right away.

"I know Hettie Robinson left that apple there."

I shrugged.

"And I see how Gillis treats you. If I had my foot back, I'd give him a lesson. In manners."

"Don't," I said. "Get your learning while you canh."

Darrel paused to shift his weight off his crutch for a few seconds' rest.

"I will," he said, charging forward again. "For as long as I have to. But you don't have to keep going for my sake. If Lucas will keep driving me, you don't need to go."

"I wantt to learn," I reminded him.

He gave me a sly look, his freckled imp's face smiling like it once did more often.

"Don't see why it matters so much now," he said, poking me with his crutch. "What does a housewife need with reading?"

And he took off hop-stepping before I could wallop him.

XLVI.

All afternoon I fret and pace, worrying about you, until even Mother remarks upon it. She says aloud, repeatedly, what a relief it is to have that horse and its big mouth gone. I wonder what she'd say if she could find another place to stable me.

At last I can't bear it and I go outside. I gather fallen limbs from the woods to replenish the woodpile. The heavy snow brought down plenty of branches. After half an hour of hauling, I've rebuilt the pile well, and I let my gathering take me in the direction of your house. Jip and your mule and sheep need tending.

I linger there as long as I dare, in hopes you may return tonight. But at length, the cold and the falling dark chase me home. Perhaps you intend to stay the night at your father's cabin. I fear that's unwise, though. Your absence could attract attention.

XLVII.

Back home I open the door and see Rupert Gillis seated at our table, nursing a cup of ale and trying to engage Darrel in conversation. Mother ignores him, of course, and goes about her supper chores. It's too late for me to pretend I didn't see him. I go in. Mother's expression changes.

"Ah! Daughter," Mother says. Darrel and I both look at her strangely. "Just in from your chores. What a hard worker you are."

Still in my coat, I sink into a chair, utterly bewildered.

"Come, Darrel," Mother says. "It's time you took a bit of exercise outdoors. Let me help you to the barn. There's something there I would show you."

Darrel protests but Mother drowns him out and propels him toward the door. He meets my gaze.

Don't leave me!

He has no choice.

The door shuts behind them.

"A tender and beautiful thing, is a mother's love for her daughter," Gillis says.

I refuse to look at him.

"Her love makes her hope against all reason that I might become your suitor."

Suitor indeed.

The silence stretches out like cold molasses.

The schoolmaster moves his chair so he sits directly in front of me. I look at my lap.

"But I imagine you have hopes of another suitor," he says. "Hopes that are even more absurd than your mother's hopes for you."

He bends low so his jeering face is beneath my own. I close my eyes. "Lucas Whiting would never take you for his own." He laughs. Then he grows serious. "I would make an honest woman out of you. I always did think silence was a womanly virtue."

My teeth are clenched. I will not look at him.

"My home is comfortable. You should not let foolish hopes deny you your one chance of respectability."

He waits for me to reconsider. I rise from my seat and stand by the fire with my back toward him.

His breathing is angry now. He rises from his seat and yanks my arm so that I must face him.

"If you think our war hero would ever settle for a used mute, you are a fool."

His words sting, and my eyes grow wet. Please, dim light, hide me, let me yield nothing to this fiend.

"Not that it matters now. The war hero is soon to fall."

I open my eyes.

There is triumph in his.

"Do you know where he is now? Perhaps he told you he had to race off to find his father's cabin, before the search party left in a few days." He laughs more. "Sharing confidences. How quaint. Your fancy lad is a worse fool than you."

I can't help it; I look up at him. His spectacled eyes bulge with cruel mirth.

"It was a trap. They let him hear of the expedition to see if he'd go on his own. And when he left this morning, they followed him. By now he'll have led them right to Colonel Whiting's hideaway."

Oh, Lucas! Phantom, lose yourself and Lucas in the woods but do not go to your old home!

Nothing I can do veils the panic in my eyes. Rupert Gillis delights in it. If he couldn't woo me, he's had his pleasure wounding me.

He takes a long, noisy gulp of his ale. Mother's best, which she keeps for company. He smacks his lips.

"No telling what they'll do to him when they catch him."

I watch the bubbles in his ale pop.

"Or what they've already done to him."

I hear voices outside, then a noise at the door. Darrel opens it and hobbles inside, Mother at his heels. She pains on a forced smile.

"Care to stay for dinner, Mr. Gillis?" she says.

"Thank you, no," he says. He sets his mug down on the mantelpiece over the fire. "I've stayed too long as it is. Miss Finch." He bows for my benefit.

XLVIII.

Once more I wait for Mother and Darrel to go to sleep. I dress silently and slip out the door, praying I won't encounter the intruder who's been lurking around our house.

I can't cross the river in the dark, alone. It's running high from melted snow. If you can take my horse, I will take your mule. I visit our barn on my way and fill my pockets with apples to persuade her to come with me.

I slip a harness over her, lead her into your barnyard, and tether her to a fence post so I can try to mount her. She brays so loud I fear Goody Pruett will wake, never mind Mother. But at length, after several apples and bruises, I'm seated on her back, and I lead her out onto the path toward the river.

The river rushes high, black and bottomless in the moonless night.

She balks at entering the water, as I knew she would.

If I knew she would, why didn't I form a plan?

I coax. I nudge with my feet and slap her side. She won't enter the river. I dismount and offer her apples, dangling them out over the water. She can lean farther than I can. In despair I try to push her from behind. She won't go.

There's nothing left. I strip off my shoes and all of my clothes and tie them in a bundle on her shoulders. It's not cold enough to freeze the river, but cold enough to freeze me. The wind that felt so inviting when I left my house is deadly now. And I haven't even touched the water.

I start with one foot.

Cold! Cold. So cold it's hot. It burns. I can't. I can't.

I pull back and think.

Lucas, Lucas, why didn't you see this was a trap? Why didn't I? What was I thinking?

Out there in the wilderness, they might bypass your trial and administer their own justice. An eye for an eye won't leave you with much.

I grab hold of the mule's tether rope, feed her my last apple, and plunge into the water.

XLIX.

Suicide. Cold. Pain, pain, never such pain.

Only seconds to go before . . . already I can't feel my hands.

The mule comes along. Makes no sense. There's no sense in this cold.

Cold, slimy rocks on the bottom tear my bare feet. The mule follows.

Slick gravel slides beneath me and my head goes under. Cold in my mouth and throat. Too cold for fear.

The mule swims beside me and drags me along, bashing my knees into rocks on the far side. My feet are past feeling but my legs try to stand. I stumble ashore, streaming water and blood.

I collapse on the riverbank, white and naked like the first Io. The mule lies down beside me, drenched with cold water but steaming out heat.

L.

My clothes are dry. A miracle. I scrape water off my frozen skin and pull the clothes on with frigid fingers. I squeeze the water from my hair. I can't mount the mule now, but it's just as well. I must move to warm myself. I lead her along through the woods in the dark, and she follows me, placid as a lamb.

I walked this trail the very first night, and he led me as I now lead the mule. I couldn't bear to look at him for the sight of what was draped over his shoulders. White hands hung down, flapping with each step, and a head bobbed against his back, baring her white and bruised neck.

I've made this journey several times now.

Lottie went this way only once.

LI.

Time passes without my knowing. My feet follow the unseen trail, and your mule follows me. It's dark, but I don't get lost. My clothes feel wonderfully warm after my naked bath.

Here is the gap. I tether the mule loosely to a tree and slide down the incline that appears, to those who don't know, to end in a rock face. I feel around until I find the opening, and then I'm through.

A hundred more yards of clawing my way through branches, and I'm at the edge of the clearing of what was to be my home.

I smell wood smoke. I hear movement. I circle around.

Light streams from the window. My window, where I watched the moon.

It takes me a moment to realize what I see where the light falls outside.

Tied to a tree is a man's limp body.

Yours.

LII.

Years of silence prevent my screaming.

Shadows pass before the window. Men with lit candles, searching the house, low voices reaching through the wooden slats.

I circle around the clearing, taking care never to come into view. Could there be guards? I find none. I creep up behind you and touch your hands, lashed behind you. They're cold, but not the cold of death. They twitch.

Thank heaven. I lean against the tree for a moment.

You're sagging against the ropes that bind you to the tree trunk. You wear no coat. Why didn't I bring a knife? I tear at the knots.

"Who's there?"

I kiss your hand.

"Judith?" You sound weak. "What are you doing here?"

I creep around the tree to look you in the eye. You look terrible. Your face is bruised, one eyebrow swollen, and your clothes are torn in several places, showing scraped limbs underneath. You shiver in the cold air.

"Watch out, they'll see you. The window."

One look tells me you're freezing to death. With flat hands I rub your body in fast circles. You shudder at my touch. It hurts you.

"They'll see you!" This time there's no ignoring your urgency. I go back behind the tree to loosen your knots.

"Did they beatt you?"

You almost laugh. "I didn't want to be captured, but Horace Bron had different ideas."

Horace Bron is a mountain of a man. "You're lucky you're alive."

"Judith, I should have suspected. They followed me. I came into the house, and they ambushed me."

I can picture this too clearly. "I know."

Your voice breaks. "You knew?"

I come back around the tree to face you. How could you doubt me so? "Gillis came over tonightt to gloatt."

"Gillis!" You spit. "He was the one who told me 'the secret.'"

"Shhh," I warn, for your voice is rising. These knots are stubborn, and in the dark I have little success. You twist and struggle against your bonds, as if now that I'm here they'll yield.

This never should have happened! "I *told* you there was nothing here to worry aboutt."

The moon breaks through a gap in the clouds. I see it through the same trees that I watched for two years.

Enough of this. You're already suffering enough without me proving I was right.

"Where's Phanttom?"

"Loose. She ran off, and they haven't found her." One thing to be glad about.

"Judith," you tell me, "don't untie me. Find Phantom and go home."

I didn't come this far for Phantom.

"They'll kill you," I whisper. "I'm nott going."

"They won't kill me. They're bringing me back to town tomorrow for a public hearing."

"How can you be shhure?"

"I heard them talking. William Salt says he's found some-thing of Lottie's that proves my father killed her."

What?

What kind of thing?

I remember Lottie dying. I picture it once more. I feel like I've jumped back into the river.

I think carefully about what I'm about to say. "He didn't kill Lottie, Lucass."

Do you believe me? I peer around the tree trunk for a glimpse of your face. Your eyes are shut. You look like you're praying. Tied to a tree, you look like Jesus on the cross in Bible pictures.

"Then who did kill her?" I can barely hear you.

Now I know you won't believe me. "I don't know."

The awful silence stretches on.

I can no longer see shadows moving before the window. The candle's light snuffs out. Are they going to sleep and leaving you here? I wonder why there are no guards out here watching you, but these impenetrable knots are reason enough.

"Judith," you say softly, "if I could escape these ropes, and I asked you to come away with me, ride on Phantom and set out west, tonight, would you come?"

The darkness makes me bold. I abandon the knots and stand inches before you.

"And if we weren'tt running away?" I ask. "Would you have me for your wife in Roswell Station?"

You lean your face forward. Your nose touches mine. It's cold.

"I would," you say, "but let's not."

I press myself against you and hope warmth from me can find you.

LIII.

You caress my cheek against yours. "Be my wife, Judith," you say. "Please say you will."

This place. That word.

I peel myself away. "Let'ss gett you untied. You're no good to me thiss way."

I attack the knots. I'm ready to bite them.

Your wife.

"Ssh!"

You hiss through your lips. There's a sound at the door.

"Go!" you whisper.

I can't leave you!

I can't help you if I'm caught.

The door opens, and I hear heavy footsteps. Under the cover of their noise I scurry back into the darkness. The footsteps stop.

"Ho there!" It's the voice of William Salt, the miller. I abandon stealth and run.

Crashing footsteps follow me. Stinging nettles and branches lash my face. My eyes water. The cold air makes my chest ache.

I twist my ankle on a tree root. Still I run. The moon retreats and the darkness is choking. I've lost all sense of where I am. The footsteps draw closer. Back in the distance I hear shouts. The other men, I suppose. My body can't go any faster, my ankle throbs with each step.

I stop.

And so does my pursuer.

He can't find me without my movements to follow.

I can't still my breath after such a mad race.

More rumblings in the distance of shouting voices near the house. Orange light begins to shine through the trees. Could they have built a bonfire so quickly?

The flames rise higher.

William Salt turns back and wades through the undergrowth toward the fire.

That's no bonfire. They're burning the colonel's house.

At least you'll be warm.

My body, damp with sweat, begins to chill in the night air. Now I can hear the crackling of the burning house.

Burning house.

Gunpowder.

What if it wasn't all removed from the cellar?

LIV.

They must have removed it. They must. Or there would have been an explosion by now. One that would dwarf the exploding homelander ships. No, in their search they must have found and removed it. They wouldn't go to this trouble to recover their arsenal only to burn it now.

Phantom appears and nuzzles my ear. Good girl.

I'm desperate to think of a way to rescue you. But how, with everyone on alert?

I try to climb up on Phantom. She bends herself down, and with the help of a low-hung tree limb, I climb onto her back.

I can't rescue you now. I surrender you to the men for tonight.

I pat Phantom's neck. Take me home, girl, I think. She doesn't need to hear me say it. She turns toward the burning house and sniffs the air, then sets off in the other direction, toward the shale slope. I twine my fingers through her mane and rest my head against her neck.

LV.

Thank goodness, in the dark I can barely see her perilous climb. But she can. She leads me out of the valley and brings me to a shallower part of the river that I don't recognize in the dark. Without a pause she plunges in. I hoist up my skirts and my legs. She is sure-footed over the slippery rocks and never even gets her belly wet. She shakes herself off on the opposite shore and leads me through the forest until we come out onto the road, in between the village and your house. She doesn't stop until she's reached my barn. I slide off her back and lead her inside.

Io moos contentedly.

I rub Phantom down for a long time so she won't take a chill from her dip in the river. My body aches with weariness and cold, but I can't thank her enough for sparing me another swim. I throw fresh straw down into Io's stall and let Phantom in beside her. Phantom huddles next to Io. They'll keep each other warm tonight.

LVI.

It's still full dark, but the sky tingles with predawn. I approach the house and see once more, in my mind's eye, the colonel's house ablaze. That was to be my house, my refuge. You will be my refuge now. So I must get you free.

I place my hand on the door latch and lift it quietly.

It's locked.

I try it again to be sure.

Mother's face appears in the window. She sees it's me and closes the shutters.

I rattle the latch.

"Please!" I cry through the latch. "Lett me in!"

"You don't live here." Mother's voice is muffled by Father's well-made door.

Not this. Not now. I survey my filthy clothes and shivering, aching body. "Only once more," I plead. "One more time, lett me in. I'll never come back."

"Go back to the man you need so badly and see if he'll take you in."

Cold, weary, and frightened to death, rejected by the mother who nursed me. It is more than I can bear. My eyes fill with tears, my throat with sobs.

"Mercy for a daughtter," I cry, pounding at the door. "Mother, help me!"

I hear Darrel's voice but can't make out the words. Mother makes a sound, and it silences him.

The house stands dark and still. The site of all my happier memories of Father, and Mother in better times, its blackened boards are unmoved by my distress.

I back away from it.

I bid my father's house good-bye.

One last time in the barn, I scratch Io's head, then lead Phantom out. She whickers her protest; she's just gotten comfortable. But she follows me to your barn, where she and I lie back to back on a bed of straw.

Only then do I remember your mule. May she find her own way back. I can't help her now.

BOOK FOUR

I.

I wake to clamor. The church bell rings again and again, sounds the alarm, summoning the entire village to come at a run. Homelanders? I wipe my eyes and look around me, dazed.

It's midmorning. I missed my chores.

Still the bell clangs.

I'm in your barn, with Jip curled up against my belly.

Now I remember.

I jump up to find my bruised legs wobbly underneath me. I hold on to the stall while I pluck the straw off my rumpled dress. My belly growls. Phantom noses me for her feed. Oats for her you have, but nothing that will feed me, and your house is locked.

The bell rings for you, and for the explorers' return. It must be that. I won't know anything unless I go and listen myself. I'll hide in my rear corner as usual. Perhaps in this moment of crisis I'll be noticed even less.

I set off down the path. Up ahead, making slow but dignified progress up the road, are Mother in her Sunday best, and Darrel, leaning on her arm. Darrel didn't go to school, it seems. Couldn't, with no one to help him. I hang back behind a maple tree and wait for them to get far beyond me.

"Playing hidey-tag?"

I jump. It's Goody Pruett. She cackles at my skittishness.

"You're a wreck, aren't you? What happened to your clothes? And how come you're hiding from your own mother?"

She pats me on the elbow, and somehow I find myself escorting her by the arm into town.

"Don't take too much imagination to think of a reason. Old Goody Pruett's been around a long time, she has."

She walks so slowly I despair of arriving before the meeting is over.

"Goody Pruett knows things Preacher Frye and Doc Brands don't need to know." She chortles with laughter, then peers at me with her glossy black eyes. "You're in trouble, aren't you, lassie?" She eyes the front of my dress.

I am too tired to protest my innocence. Goody joins a long list of authorities on the subject of my immorality.

We are the last ones to approach the church. Goody makes her way up the aisle, and I slip into the back. Not unnoticed. Reverend Frye's eyes follow me, as do some others, I assume from the expedition, who stand in front with guns at their sides. This room is not a church today. It's a courthouse.

You are tied to a chair next to the pulpit. Your clothes are even more soiled and tattered in the light of day. I see blood from a cracked lip, and the purple bruise around your eye. Your head droops. Everyone whispers at the sight of their disgraced young knight. Not Maria, though. She sits tight next to Leon, pale and silent.

You lift your head and search the room until you find me. I am here. I see you.

Reverend Frye thumps his cane against the floor like Moses striking the rock. The room is silenced. Five aldermen rise from the benches and take their seats on the platform. Their black robes rustle as they walk. They seem out of place in this late morning sunlight that streams through the south windows.

Horace Bron seizes your chair and turns it around to face the aldermen. He taps your cheeks to rouse you and make you look at the men.

Alderman Brown clears his throat.

"People of Roswell Station," he begins in a voice made rusty with age, "we are here to examine disturbing charges." He peers over the rim of his spectacles at you.

This provocative start to such a solemn occasion sends waves throughout the room.

"It was a shock to our village to learn that Ezra Whiting had not died years ago, as was believed, but was living in concealment nearby."

Abijah Pratt's jaw won't stop grinding. He sits in the front pew, near the wall, his body angled so he can stare at you. His thick lower lip thrusts forward and back, and his gnarled hands grip the top of his walking stick.

Alderman Brown shuffles his papers. "It began to shed light on a number of tragedies our village has suffered. It also raised the question of who knew of his whereabouts, who concealed him, and who aided him in pillaging us."

Mother's face is unmoving.

Reverend Frye, seated with the panel, interjects, "Our defenses! Our children's lives, their bodies, their purity!"

Alderman Brown's mouth tightens. He doesn't appreciate the interruption.

Strange how my body and its purity have become the town's sacred possessions, yet they spare *me* no pity. It's as if they were the ones wronged, not me.

Alderman Brown continues. "But to be sure of these charges, a party was sent across the river to locate Whiting's home and see what proofs could be found. Not only did this party find Whiting's home, but they found Whiting's son there."

Well. A rather slanted view of affairs. But factually accurate, all the same.

"He stands accused of willfully concealing Ezra during his lifetime, and assisting him in his crimes, which include theft, rapine, murder, torture, and dismemberment.

"William Salt. Will you state for the assembly here, what other items you found in Whiting's cabin?"

The miller reads from a list. "Eight kegs and twelve cases of powder. Forty-two assorted pieces of loose arms. Household items: pots, knives, blankets, clothing, some male, some female. A dress"—here he holds up a rumpled and motheaten piece of brown wool—"belonging to the deceased, Charlotte Pratt."

Charlotte. I never thought of Lottie as Charlotte.

I stare at the dress. I remember her wearing it. I remember her alive in it. I once envied its wide, round collar. Now it hangs like a dishrag, white lace yellowed with age. But something's odd. That collar, that dress . . . Could my memory be muddled?

"Abijah Pratt, do you swear that this dress belonged to your daughter?"

Finally a use for his restless, wet lips. "I do. It was her mother's. My wife sewed it herself before our crossing, when she died."

Some of the older women in town nod their heads. They wouldn't forget a piece of handiwork like that.

Alderman Brown continues. "Dr. Brands, will you describe for the assembly, the state of the body of Charlotte Pratt when it was found?"

Melvin Brands rises from his seat. "The deceased young woman's body was badly bruised and waterlogged. It was unclear whether she drowned or was dead when she entered the river."

I wonder whether Dr. Brands examined Lottie's body in ways her father wouldn't have sanctioned.

"And her state of dress?"

Dr. Brands lowers his voice. "She wore no clothes."

A murmur passes through the congregation. For shame! Cunning exhibitionism. They all knew this already.

The murmurs and whispers in the congregation grow agitated. Alderman Brown bangs a gavel on the table before him.

"We have established beyond doubt that Ezra Whiting was the abductor and murderer of Charlotte Pratt."

No.

I feel oddly removed from myself, like a sparrow lodged in the rafters, watching with one bright eye while my body stands here and my mind spins elsewhere.

But my mind, what little of it I can muster, doesn't understand. Why beyond doubt? How does a dress remove doubt? It only adds to my doubt.

You twist your head from side to side, trying to look behind you. Are you looking for me, dear heart?

"Lucas Whiting," Alderman Brown intones, and all the room falls still. "You are charged with concealing your father's whereabouts, failing to report him when his crimes were known, and supporting him in activities that threatened our safety. How do you plead?"

It's an effort for you to speak. "Innocent." Your voice is tired. "I never knew where my father was."

Abijah Pratt rises to his feet. "Who knows but what he didn't assist his father in abducting my Lottie! Taken from me in the flower of her youth!" His voice breaks into racking sobs. His grief, so raw after all these years, moves the assembly. A woman to his left hands him a handkerchief.

That *you* were part of her disappearance and death! Can anyone support such madness?

Leon Cartwright stands with some difficulty. "Alderman Brown," he says, "may I speak?"

Alderman Brown nods his head.

Leon wipes his forehead. "Gentlemen," he begins, "I wish to speak for Lucas Whiting's character. I can't believe he would have helped abduct those girls. In all his years here he's been an upstanding citizen and brother to us."

You crane your neck around to catch a glimpse of Leon.

He goes on. "A hardworking farmer, a generous neighbor. He led the victory at the gorge that saved us all." He clutches and releases the hem of his jacket. "We were both little more than lads when the girls went missing. I could never believe that of him." He turns about and takes note of all the eyes watching him. "I guess that's it." He sits down heavily, and Maria weaves her arm through his.

"The victory at the gorge was won with Ezra Whiting's help," Reverend Frye says. "Who brought the father there, if not the son?"

No one speaks.

He points a finger at you. "Well, Mr. Whiting? Who brought your father to the battle?"

You say nothing. Oh, my heart. You say nothing.

Alderman Brown half rises from his seat and scans the congregation with his eyes. They rest upon me.

"Miss Judith Finch," he calls. "Come forward."

All heads turn to locate me, except yours. And Mother's.

For a moment, I consider bolting out the door. But I'm too weak, too hungry and tired to get far before they'd overtake me.

I rise to my feet. Somehow they carry me past all those eyes to the front of the church until I'm right behind you. I can smell you. You need a bath. So do I.

Remember, I tell myself. Silence is my power. I fold my hands in front of me and look down at the floor.

"Miss Finch," Alderman Brown says. "Was it Ezra Whiting who abducted you and cut out your tongue?"

I keep my hands folded and my eyes downcast.

"She can't speak." Goody Pruett's voice makes everyone jump. I turn to look back. She's so short that even when she rises, her head is barely above those around her. For a woman to speak unbidden in any assembly is forbidden, but Goody Pruett is old enough to defy them.

"She can so!" Abijah Pratt cries. "I heard her! Just the other night! Got spooked and called out, 'Who's there?' She's been posing as a mute when she ain't! She says nothing now because she's guilty!"

Abijah Pratt was the one in our yard? What was *he* doing there? What did he want? I remember his frightening words on Maria's wedding day. *Adultery, and confession, and punishment . . .*

I spared you twice.

The brown dress they found.

I look back at Abijah Pratt, and he turns away. Not far off I see short, stocky Mr. Robinson, and inwardly I apologize for suspecting him.

I look up at the aldermen, who sit staring at Abijah. "Guilty of what, Pratt?" one of them asks. "Miss Finch is not accused of anything."

Abijah's lower lip churns the air. He turns and points at my mother. "Ask her! Miz Finch! Didn't you testify that when your girl went missing in the night, all those years back, there was no sign of anyone breaking in and taking her? That she would have had to leave the house on her own?"

I turn to watch. My mother does not acknowledge the question. Her face is a flint.

"That's what she said back then," Abijah says. "Which means the Finch girl went with Ezra of her own free will."

I feel punched in the stomach.

"*My* Lottie was virtuous. Not a man-chaser."

It's almost comical. Virtuous Lottie, and man-chasing Judith.

I hear a shuffle of feet. "Excuse me," says a voice I know too well. "If I may, I have some information that may be pertinent."

I don't turn to see. I don't want to watch Rupert Gillis say whatever he's about to.

"I fear that Lucas Whiting may indeed be falsely accused," he begins in words as precise as penmanship. "I do not believe he knew his father's whereabouts before the battle."

Hope leaps in my breast. Could Rupert Gillis's words ever be welcome to my ears?

"On the day of the battle with the homelanders, I saw Judith Finch approach Lucas Whiting and beckon him to come with her. He followed, by all appearance unwillingly, and she led him to Ezra Whiting."

So smooth, his voice, like singing. Words pour from his lips like water.

"Of course I did not know Mr. Whiting Senior, by sight, but she led Lucas to the man who burned the homelander ships."

"See?" Abijah Pratt hops from one foot to the other. "She's in league with young Whiting!"

Rupert Gillis coughs lightly. "I beg pardon," he says. "Lucas Whiting seemed entirely astonished to see his father. Like one seeing a ghost. To that I'll swear."

"So Lucas Whiting is innocent," says a voice. Whose, I'm not sure. Others murmur their relief.

See, my love? You have some loyal friends after all.

You glance at me, and your eyes are full of worry.

"As to that," Rupert goes on, clearly enjoying himself, "I do believe Lucas Whiting was ignorant of his father's continued existence. But there is evidence to suggest that Lucas Whiting and Judith Finch are in a league of some sort."

My flesh crawls at his precise, impenetrable words.

Rupert's voice is muted, as the bearer of regrettable news. "I saw them, some weeks ago, lying together in the woods, wrapped in each other's arms."

Mrs. Robinson clamps her hands over her younger daughter's ears.

Your bound arms strain against their ropes. "That's a lie!"

I want to gag.

The room crackles with titillation.

He was there again, prying, watching? I knew the schoolmaster caught me running home from your house, but I can't bear that he saw me lying with you in the woods. The lurking fiend! Has he nothing better to do with his time than haunt me?

Alderman Brown bangs his gavel. "Silence!"

An infant whimpers and claws at his mother's breast.

"That's a lie," you repeat. Your voice holds the assurance of one who knows he's falsely accused. "You slander both me and Miss Finch."

"Look at her face and tell whether he does," says one of the aldermen.

Too late, I turn my head away.

You take a deep breath to attack these charges, and then you pause.

Yes.

The blankets.

Now you know.

"What is more," Rupert Gillis adds, his voice less restrained, "as for Miss Judith Finch's character, just yesterday, during the students' dinner break, she offered to come to my house last night."

You stiffen in your seat.

"*If* I would pay her."

Roswell Station has no more room for astonishment. They sit in silent dread of God's judgment upon them for allowing me to remain in their midst. Mr. Robinson's pale eyebrows stand out against his crimson face.

Your head hangs low. You look only at your lap.

Rupert Gillis's throat is long, and white, and soft as cheese. Please look at me, Lucas.

"That's not true!" Darrel's voice rings through the wagging tongues. "She was with me all during dinner break. She's never spoken a word to Gillis! He's the one that's pestered her!"

I seek out his eyes. Thank you, Darrel. But the murmuring in the room shows no one believes a brother defending his sister's honor.

They are not my concern. Lucas, look in my eyes and see the truth.

I am accused more by you not looking at me than by them glaring. My guilt was firm in their minds the moment my name was called, the moment my tongue was cut. But you might have believed in me.

"Judith Finch," says Alderman Brown's voice from miles away. "Do you have anything to say?"

I see the sun in the highest curve of the church's tall, arched window. Such a bright, clear day. So radiant, this whitewashed room at midday.

Do I have anything to say?

Only to you.

"Judith Finch," he repeats. "Not only are you now charged with all that Lucas Whiting faced, but you are also charged with fornication and whoredom. How do you plead?"

My mother's face leaps out from the crowd at me. Her eyes are closed. She is so still, she might almost be asleep.

My defiance annoys them, but the aldermen will not show it with all the village watching.

"Lucas Whiting," says Alderman Brown, "if you were unaware of your father's whereabouts, how did you find his cabin last night?"

"My father's mare led me to it." The aldermen must lean over their table in order to hear you.

"The horse Judith Finch had brought back from the battle?"

You will not answer this. It doesn't matter. No one doubts who Phantom is.

The aldermen confer among themselves for a long moment. There is no sound but the shuffling of feet against wood. I watch William Salt bounce up and down on his heels, eyeing me sideways. Go on, tell them you saw me trying to free Lucas last night. But he doesn't. He doesn't want to admit that he couldn't capture a girl.

The aldermen finish their deliberations. "It appears, Lucas Whiting," Alderman Brown says, "that you were as ignorant of your father's existence as we were. Therefore the charges of conspiring and concealing him are dropped. However, you stand accused of fornication with Judith Finch. The mute girl. How do you plead?"

The aldermen scowl collectively at the assembly. Someone is chuckling, low.

You're unsure of what to say. No one would believe you against Gillis's testimony.

The gavel bangs. "Since you have both refused to answer the charges brought against you, your guilt must be inferred, and your punishment dealt. For fornication you will both spend three hours in the pillory, after which you will be brought to prison. In the morning, Lucas Whiting will be released. Judith Finch, for concealing Ezra Whiting from us, and the knowledge that he had raided the arsenal before destroying it, you are charged with treason and treachery. You are also accused of whoredom. Your sentence will come in the morning."

The village rises to its feet to the sound of scattered applause and whispers.

Horace Bron's heavy hands are stronger than chains around my wrist. He looks as if he wishes someone else had his bailiff's duties at this moment.

He leads me down the aisle. Schoolboys jeer and insult me, and their parents do not stop them. Mother looks away when I pass. Mrs. Robinson shoots hateful darts my way. I can't shake the sight of Abijah Pratt's malevolent eyes. I turn back for a last sight of you in your chair, but the crowd spilling from its seats has swallowed you up.

II.

With a heavy hand against the back of my head, Horace pushes me into the pillory. My wrists lie in two grooves in the wood, my neck in the larger center groove, and the upper board drops into place. My feet stand upon the platform, but my back bends awkwardly.

At least it's a warm day for November, with the sun at its peak in the sky.

If I raise my head I can see the green, the church, the school, the streets and houses. Tall evergreens rim the village, and naked trees whose yellow-brown leaves lie underfoot. Two hundred or so villagers, with children weaving in between their knees, huddle in conversation.

About me.

I let my head drop. The gray boards of the platform fill my vision. The wood beneath my neck constricts my breathing; when I lift my head my back protests.

Horace Bron goes back into the church and returns moments later with you on a lead like a colt. Your face is haggard, unshaven, and bruised. Look at me, Lucas, but don't see me this way, strung up like a carcass.

You do look at me. Until they stuff you into holes like mine, you look at me, but what is in your eyes, I cannot tell. The upper slab falls down upon you. And now the thick mast that supports the double pillory stands between us. We're feet apart but we can't see each other. Only the town can see us, pinned here like hunting trophies.

My wrists grow sore already, and I've only been here a quarter of an hour.

Caleb Wills, Dougal's lanky little brother, grows daring.

He scoops up a handful of mud and flings it at me. It splatters on the boards next to me, sprinkling my face. Caleb waits for someone to restrain him, then gleefully scoops another ball. This time his aim is better.

It is some time before I can open my eyes.

I hear the boys' whoops as they run off. I know they'll be back.

They return with handfuls of compost. Cabbages and peppers grown weepy with rot. I can smell them before they throw them at me. Foul, corrupted apples and potatoes, still hard enough to sting on impact. Nor are you spared.

They pelt us while their parents gaze on.

Then:

"That's enough," Horace Bron roars. All the brats retreat to their mothers' skirts. All the townsfolk remember work that needs doing. As quickly as it began, it ends, and everyone flaps off to gnaw on our bones from a safer distance.

III.

Horace Bron returns to his smithy, which faces the common. He can work and watch us at the same time.

Still more than two hours remaining, and no relief to anticipate when this is done.

I wonder what the French girl felt, tied to the stake, while her countrymen kindled flames at her feet. Relief, perhaps, that it would soon be over?

My eyes sting with the cold and with the refuse that splashed them.

My back aches.

But not as much as other things.

IV.

We stand. We droop. We stand again.

We twist our necks so the sinews bear some of the head weight, and not our windpipes.

I can't see you but I feel your movements through the pillory beams.

We don't speak. What is there to say?

V.

"I'm cold at night," he said to me one morning. "Unless you want to share my bunk, use those scraps and old things of yours to make me a blanket, since I've given you mine."

I made him a blanket.

He criticized my sewing. Mother would have done the same, I thought. And oh, how I would have loved to hear her do it.

VI.

He didn't need to lock me in that second night. I was still too frightened by all I'd seen, and by the man who had threatened me, to think of escape. Such thoughts and boldness came later.

But he locked me in anyway. He said he had a delivery to make. He took something large, wrapped up in a blanket.

VII.

Lottie was in love. I knew it must be why she had run away. I worried about her, but not like others in town did. I was certain she was alive, hiding somewhere with her fella. I hoped she'd come tell who the boy was. She was sure she'd be married soon.

Love brought her no better luck than it has brought me.

VIII.

I picture the dress, dangling from the miller's hand. So imp
and crumpled, faded and devoured. It is strange to me to
think that I once envied her that dress. I thought about that
even during my years with him. How ironic it was that I
had once envied Lottie her two fancy dresses. Much good
they did her. Even so, I thought about the brown one, so
elegant, nothing like the dress I wore out until he replaced it.
Its beauty was long faded.

How little do things like dresses truly matter, then or now.

IX.

What was Abijah Pratt doing outside my house with a lantern? Why would he still hate me so? Lottie died long ago.

"Judith."

The voice seems to come from far away.

"Judith. Are you all right?"

The back of my neck bangs against the top plank of the
pillory.

You. You're speaking to me.

"Um-hmm," I answer. "You?"

I can only imagine how you must look in the pillory.

"I can think of other places I'd rather be."

My laugh is weak.

"Not I," I say. "I love it here."

You laugh, and for a moment I could forget where we are.
But the laughter dies away, and we're left no closer.

"I'm sorry," you say.

"Why?"

You aren't finding words. "For . . ."

"For thinking you mightt love me?"

"What do you mean?" You sound angry.

"Nothing," I say. "Ssorry."

Your anger rises. "What?"

"Doesn't matter, Lucass," I say. "I'll be dead by tomorrow noon. Find anyone you will, marry her and raise a dozen babies."

"What do you *mean*, you'll be dead by tomorrow noon?"

I rotate my head from side to side, searching for a comfortable spot. "They won't restt until they can blame someone for Lottie." Oh no, don't cry now! "Now that I'm a wantton and a whore, I'm no loss."

All I can hear is the sound of your breathing. Supper smells begin to drift from village chimneys.

"Judith."

"Mm?"

"Judith. Listen to me."

Something in your voice stops me from ranting more. "I am."

"I love you."

Oh, help.

"Since I was a boy I've loved you. Do you believe me?"

I'm waylaid by tears that aren't from the cold. And I have no way to wipe them off my nose.

Your voice is warm and loving. "I need you to believe me."

I sniffle. "I do."

"Good," you say. Your voice changes. "Then I'm going to tell them that I did help my father abduct Lottie Pratt."

"No!"

Horace Bron looks up from his anvil across the way.

"No," I repeat with more control.

"I'll do it," you say. "And you will go free."

"No I won't," I cry. "They won't let me go free."

You are silent for a time. "Then, if not that, when they release me I'll find a way to rescue you."

"Oh? And then whatt?"

"Then we'll ride away on Phantom and start our life together." You sniff. The cold has congested you. "Maybe we can find my mother."

Oh, my dear. You still think of her. Of course you do.

"Why do you sound reluctant?" you ask. "Don't you love me?"

Let me not weep any longer. Not in this place.

"Lucass," I say, "would you love me if your father had . . . forssed himself upon me?"

You do not hesitate. "Yes," you say, bravely and well. I pause to savor what this means.

"And if I'd . . . forssed myself upon you, that night in the woods?" I almost smile, imagining your discomfiture.

"Yes," you say, not without embarrassment.

I can barely bring myself to say these words. "And if I had triedd to sedusse Rupertt Gilliss?"

You're quiet a long time. "I would still love you," you say slowly, "but it would be hard to overlook that."

I'm pilloried in the center of town, torn and tattered, and smiling. The sun begins its descent in the sky, and I'm chilled to the bone, but I'm happy. I wait for a gawking child to pass before I speak.

"Would you believe me," I ask, watching up and down the street for anyone to come by, "if I said none of it happened?"

How I wish I could see your face.

In the west, clouds pile on the horizon. The air grows colder.

Blood's not flowing to my fingers properly anymore.

"None of it?"

"None."

At first I assume you're pondering this, until I feel the pillory boards shaking.

You're crying! "My . . . father didn't hurt you?"

There is no need for me to protect you from him anymore.

"He cutt out my tongue. But he never forssed me." This word is the one good thing I've gotten from knowing Rupert Gillis.

Your crying dries up. "Then he did this to you."

"He was inssane, Lucass," I say. "He said it was to protect me. He also said it when he first took me away."

"Protect you from what?" you ask.

I am not sure how to answer this question. I have never been sure. "It was a disstortion," I say. "A lie. His great fear was being discovered. He said my ssilence would protectt me, but it only protectted him."

This troubles you for a time. I understand.

"And the schoolmaster?" you ask.

This question angers me, and I don't try to hide it. And the ache in my back is now a stabbing pain. "Lucass. Am I a whore?"

"No." At least you sound sure of yourself.

I must be strict with you. You've insulted my judgment. "How couldh I *ever* favor Rupertt Gilliss?"

I hear you chafing against the neck opening of the pillory.

"He's so . . . educated. Good with books and speaking. Someone like you would fancy that."

I am too shocked to reply well. I laugh out loud. "Is *that* what you think?"

"Well, isn't that why you went to school?"

Incredible.

I think of Gillis's ruler stinging my hand. "I wentt to learn. And help Dharrel." You sniff some more. I still can't believe it. "You thoughtt I wentt to be near *Gilliss?*"

You actually thought so! And you're piqued with me, even.

You clear your throat. "When Mother left, she . . ." This is painful for you. "Her beau was a scholar. Aiming to teach."

X.

The church bell strikes the hour. Two o'clock. We have another hour to go. I'm cold in every place I can be cold. I wonder if I'll last the hour. Yet it cannot end. These will be my last moments with you.

You spoke of escape, but you're as bone-weary and famished as I am.

How will they kill me? I wonder. Stoning? Hanging? No such thing has happened in Roswell Station in my lifetime.

"Judith," you say, "did you speak truly when you told me that my father had not killed Lottie Pratt?"

What I'd give to rub my neck. "I never liedh to you, Lucass."

I see a speck approaching slowly on the long westward road, coming from the direction of your house and mine. What used to be mine. I watch it move to pass the time.

It's Goody Pruett, carrying something in a basket. The

sun moves faster across the sky than poor Goody can walk down the road.

"Then how did he come to have her dress in his house?"

I'd been wondering that myself. There must have been something confused in my memory. When he brought her body to the house, and then, when he took her to the river . . .

Goody Pruett approaches and crosses the common to where we are. When she tries to climb the steps to the platform, Horace Bron sees her and runs out to help her up.

"What is it, Mrs. Pruett?" he asks.

"Got soup for them," she says. "They're spent, and it's much too cold to stand still this long. They need something to warm their bellies."

The smell of the soup reaches my nostrils, and my mouth fills with water. Bless Goody Pruett forever. I watch Horace, anxious at what he might say. He says nothing, though. Only looks on as she unwraps the cloth around her kettle of soup.

"Carry on, then," Horace says, jumping down off the platform. "Holler at me when you're ready to come down, and I'll fetch you." He walks away.

"Thank you, Goodhy," I say.

She eyes me sharply. "So you *can* talk."

I nod my head. Soup! Give me the soup!

She eyes me appraisingly. "Sound a bit garbled, but it's speech. I'll be darned." She clamps the kettle of soup to her side and dips a large spoon in. She tips the spoon against my lips and warm chicken broth flows in.

I know you're next to me, just as famished, but I slurp the broth hungrily, as fast as she can give it to me, until I feel the warmth inside me. Then I can close my lips when she offers more. "Now Lucass," I say.

She shuffles over to where you are. It's maddening to watch her arm raise the spoon and hear you drink, but not see your face.

"So are you sweet on her?" she asks you. Always direct, our Goody.

You gulp your soup. "Yes, ma'am."

"And why not?" She leans back to look at me. "And you're sweet on him?"

I feel my face flushing. I'm in the stocks, and *this* embarrasses me? "I am."

She feeds you another bite. "Course you are. You'd be a fool not to be. Goody Pruett was a girl once herself! Always told your mother you were no fool. Clever little slip of a thing you were. Didn't say much, but took everything in with those big cow eyes of yours."

Cow eyes. It's fitting.

She gives you more soup, then returns for a second course for me.

"So what Goody wants to know is why you didn't speak up for yourself in there. Because something's not right about this. That's plain as turnips. Something ain't right, and why didn't you say so?"

I'm at a loss. My reasons seem less clear to me now.

"They'dd never believe me," I say.

She scrapes the kettle. "You don't know that."

"Not even my mother believes me."

She gives you the last scrapings. I'm full now.

"Ah," she says, "there's a heartbroken woman for you. Loved your father like nothing Goody's seen. There's no justice in this world, the things that happen to people."

Father. I remember the way Mother's eyes watched him. Like she could never get enough. She spent her life loving him, like I've spent mine loving you.

Goody stoops to pack up her things. She stands with her basket on her arm. "So, now, Judith Finch," she says. "What does Goody Pruett do to help you?"

XI.

Horace Bron looks up from his forge and sees Goody ready to leave. He sets out across the road.

XII.

Lottie's face showed fear when he appeared, but not terror. She didn't expect to die.

XIII.

Horace is nearly here.

Now. I make myself speak.

"Ring the alarm, Ghoody. Ring the bell."

She blinks once, then offers her arm to Horace. They venture down the stairs, Goody chattering all the way.

He leads her to the road.

"What are you going to do?" you whisper.

"I'm not sure," I confess.

Goody thanks Horace and ventures off toward the church. He retreats into the smithy. Goody's slow steps seem quick enough now.

XIV.

I climbed down from the tree and tiptoed across the clearing to where Lottie's body lay. I crouched beside her and touched her neck. Her mouth was open, her tongue distended.

She looked nothing like herself. If it weren't for her dress, and what I'd seen before, I could almost wonder if it was her.

I backed away.

Then hands seized me from the back and wrapped themselves around my neck.

XV.

Goody reaches the top step and disappears through the door. Just an old widow, making afternoon prayers. It must be around half past two.

XVI.

Something crashed into us like a boulder rolling downhill. I fell to the ground, crushed under the man's weight and whatever had hit him.

It was another man. They rolled off me, struggling. The boulder man quickly overpowered the first, pressing his face into the dirt, facing away from me. I couldn't see the face.

XVII.

The church bells ring. Again and again they clang the alarm.

Doors open and villagers come streaming out, their faces astonished. Reverend Frye hurries out from Alderman Wilson's house and limps toward the church as fast as he can. What will happen to Goody, I wonder?

The bells stop ringing.

Abijah Pratt comes around a corner. He glares at us on his way into the building.

Rupert Gillis and his students come around the pillory from behind and pass us on their way to the church. We take a few pinecones flung at our backs.

Villagers pour into the church, then neat as you please, Goody Pruett slips out and makes her way down the steps. She is the only one moving against the tide, and several heads turn to watch her. They go into the church, but in a few minutes they return.

Now she stands on the grass at our feet, looking up at us expectantly. She watches me, nodding slightly, encouragement shining in her beetle eyes.

The church disgorges its occupants and they move as a body to where we are. The latecomers approaching from out of town come straight toward us.

I can't squash this panic. What have I done?

"Judith," you say. "I believe you."

XVIII.

"What is the meaning of this?" Reverend Frye demands. "Who rang the bell?" He and the aldermen have caught up with the rest of the village. Without their robes they lack some of their fearfulness. The tips of their noses are red with cold.

"I did," Goody Pruett says. "Miss Judith Finch here has something to say."

This is so unexpected that for a moment no one speaks.

I find Maria's face looking up at me intently. Her face is pale and swollen, and then I know: she's going to have a baby.

Goody Pruett's insight is rubbing off on me.

I want to kiss Maria's baby on its christening day.

I want her to kiss mine someday.

Out on the road I see Darrel and Mother approach. Mother halts when she sees the gathering on the common, and starts to turn back. Darrel grabs her arm and makes his way forward on his crutch. Mother, reluctant, follows.

"This is ridiculous," Alderman Stevens says. "We all know she can't speak."

"Pratt said she can," Alderman Brown says. "Well, young woman?"

I swallow several times, which hurts my throat. There is no turning away from their faces. I'm stuck.

That's the first problem.

"Releasse uss," I say. Mouths hang open everywhere at the shock of me talking. "I will tell you the truth aboutt Lottie Pratt's death. I was there. I ssaw it happen."

XIX.

Rupert Gillis's eyes grow wide. He doesn't favor a world in which Judith Finch can speak.

"But that's ridiculous," Abijah Pratt says. "She went missing days after Lottie did."

"But before Lottie's body was found," Dr. Brands says.

They are all a chorus of arguing voices. I hear some calling to release us, others protesting that our sentence is not yet up, still others arguing that it's nearly up.

Horace Bron steps forward and releases the latch on the upper plank. The pain in my back when I finally stand is overwhelming, but it's heaven to let my arms fall. I come

forward and lean against the pillory post for support. At last
I can see your face. Horace sets you free, too, and you stand
beside me.

Every shred of flesh in me trembles. They're all staring at
me.

The aldermen aren't happy with Horace's decision. Alderman Brown delays judgment, but his eyes never leave my face.

"Miss Finch," he says, "why have you concealed your
speech from us?"

Maria speaks up. "She hasn't, sir," she says. "I've only
just been helping her practice her sounds. Until recently she
couldn't speak at all. Or rather, she didn't know she could."

Darrel gives Mother a hard look and speaks up. "Our
mother forbade her," he says, to shocked murmurs.

"Well, Miss Finch," Alderman Brown says, "speak now,
if you ever wish to."

I feel you beside me, strengthening me.

I will speak, though my sounds are crude. I will use words
long denied to me, with no apology for how corrupt they
sound. My listeners will hear what they choose to hear.

XX.

Like the clanging of the bell, the truth crashes in upon me.

At last I understand. He took away my voice to save me.

And now, to save myself, I take it back.

XXI.

You don't touch me, but I feel your strength upholding me.

"Lottie and I were friends," I say.

I pause and look to see how they respond to my speech.

"We would talk. When she vanishedh she was fifteen. I was fourteen."

White-capped women nod their heads. They remember.

"She told me she fanssied a boy. Wouldn't say who. Talked of eloping."

I wait for this scandalous news to settle. Eyes rove about, searching for suspects.

"First I thought she *had* elopedh. But no one else was missing. Maybe she'dh only run off.

"We used to meett by a willow tree near the river. So I snuck out and waited to see if she'dh come talk to me. I hid in the branches.

"She came. I wanted to ssurprise her. So I made no noise.

"She was closse. We both heardh footstepss. A man. I couldn't see him well.

"The man attackedh Lottie. He chokedh her."

I must stop. I feel light-headed. Pressed back by all those horrified eyes upon me, the pillory is a stay and a comfort.

Abijah Pratt is openly weeping now. To dig up the dead like this . . . I hesitate. Do I do right to continue?

XXII.

"I saw his hands. Not his face. He wore a hatt.

"He left her there and ran. I waitedh.

"I keptt thinking she might wake up."

And I begin to cry. The memory is too vivid now.

Goody Pruett waves a hanky in the air, and you bend down and retrieve it for me.

"I . . . climbedh down . . . and wentt to her. That's when ssomeone . . ." I can feel the hands. ". . . attackedh me . . . and began to choke me, too."

I feel my throat begin to close and my panic rise. I draw in a slow breath. And another. You press your hand on my shoulder.

"Ssomeone came and threw him down.

"My defender was Ezra Whiting."

XXIII.

The square is buzzing. Only Goody Pruett's eyes are surprised by nothing. They watch me steadily. She nods her head. Go on. Go on.

I take a deep breath to race to the finish.

"Colonel Whiting pinned the man on the groundd. The man dared the colonel to kill him. Colonel Whiting wouldn'tt. He made the man sswear nott to harm me. Then the colonel said, he didn't trusst him a lick. So he said, 'I'm deadh. I'll take the girl. Ssee you never come where I am.' He said he'd take Lottie and make sure she was foundh in ssome other place.

"He picked up Lottie and dragged me away. We crossed the river and hiked to his cabin.

"The next day he took Lottie's dress and gave it to me. He took Lottie's body away that nightt and dropped it over the falls."

XXIV.

Isn't that the end?

I see from their eyes they want more. They want to know what happened to *me*.

We were speaking of Lottie. Very well.

"For two years I livedh with him. I tried to esscape but he always caught me."

I know what they're thinking now.

But I have the platform. They will believe my voice. I look Alderman Brown in the eye.

"I sspoke truth when I said he never harmed my maidden-hoodh. He didn't. He was tempted to, and he foughtt it. At last he couldn't fightt, sso he cutt out my tongue and ssentt me back."

Mothers clamp their hands over their mouths.

"He said he did it to protectt me. I thoughtt he was madd. But he knew the man who'd killed Lottie would remember me. I think he thoughtt by silencing me, he could save me."

I swallow.

"He was rightt."

XXV.

"But the arsenal!" Alderman Stevens calls out. "You knew of that—why didn't you tell us?"

"I didn't," I say. "Not until the homelanders came. One morning he hadd boxes and crates and barrels. He stowedd them in the cellar. I was . . . too sadd to notice much. But when I saw the village arm itsself, I understoodd. So I went to him and asked him to help at the battle. That is how he came there. Lucas didn't know."

Eunice Robinson looks visibly relieved. You are cleared

from any taint. Never mind her or any of them noticing I saved the town.

"As for the other accusations," I say, and I make no effort now to hide my anger, "they are falsse. I am a maidden sstill. I found Mr. Whiting, asleep and coldd and sick, in the forest. So I gott blankets to cover him, and I lay with him for warmth. As you ssaw, he didn't know."

"Indecent conduct," Reverend Frye says. All eyes turn toward him, and he stops.

I point to Rupert Gillis. "How *he* ssaw us there, I don't know," I said, "but ssince I entered sschool, he has abusedd me with filthy words. He told me to come to his home at nightt. He says if I don't, he'll expel me from sschool."

Gillis pretends indignation. I have never felt so powerful. "He says he likess a girl who can't tell tales."

Elizabeth Frye, the preacher's red-haired daughter, raises her hand. "I will attest to that," she says, in her spiderweb voice. "I have seen him embarrass Miss Finch, and I've received unwelcome attentions from him myself."

Reverend Frye looks strangled himself, with surprise and then anger. Poor Elizabeth may face punishment tonight. But Rupert Gillis shrinks by about six inches, and the mothers of Roswell Station gather their schoolgirls close.

"But we still don't know who killed Lottie Pratt," Alderman Brown says, frowning. "You're saying that someone among us is responsible for this?"

I step back. I feel so exposed, up here on this platform. Vulnerable to any attack. But I have come too far to crumble now.

"All I know," I say, "is that the brown dress you held was

not the dress Lottie Pratt wore when she diedd. That dress was dark blue with a triangle collar. I wore it for a year. When it . . ." I can censor my words here. ". . . tore, I ssewed it into a blankett, along with the dress I had on when I was taken, which was gray. Go look at the blankett you brought back, and you'll see both colors of wool.

"That dress was never in Colonel Whiting's housse, or I would have known," I say. "It had no reason to be there. Unless . . ."

Oh . . .

Lord have mercy.

"Unless what?" Alderman Brown says.

I swallow once more. "Unless ssomeone from the ssearch party took it there. Ssomeone who hadd the dress all along."

All eyes turn toward Abijah Pratt. His lower lip thrusts back and forth again.

"Ssomeone who has sstalkedd our house, since the battle at the gorge, when my protector diedd. Hasn't he, Mother?"

My mother blanches with surprise, then nods her head. She paid attention at the trial, too.

"Lottie was afraidd of how her father would react if he knew she was ssweet on a boy," I said. "I never knew how much reason she hadd."

XXVI.

Abijah Pratt turns around suddenly, as if to run away, and collides with the human rock wall, Horace Bron, who lifts him as easily as he would a child.

Reverend Frye stands gripping Elizabeth's arm, his mouth opening and closing like a catfish's.

Alderman Brown is watching me. I return his gaze. His eyes seem older now. His beard bends against his chest as he bows his head gravely, then looks up at me once more. He turns and fixes a sterner gaze upon Rupert Gillis, who swallows hard. Without a word, Alderman Brown turns and walks away, and the other aldermen follow. Horace Bron pushes Abijah Pratt after them, shackling his prisoner's wrists with only his massive hand. Gillis watches them go, then retreats another way, and I wonder whether he'll soon spend time in this pillory, or find a way to slip out of town tonight.

Goody Pruett's dried-apple face beams at me. She raises her hands high and claps them in the air. Again and again, until a few other hands slowly pick up the applause. Leon Cartwright's hands. Darrel's.

Maria looks ready to burst with pride.

I fear my knees will buckle beneath me and I'll drop to the platform like a fallen dress.

My mother elbows her way forward. She looks up at me, then looks away.

Maria mounts the steps of the platform, holding the rail tight. "Come home with me, Judith," she says. "Let me feed you and clean you up."

Maria puts her arm through mine, and I remember the filth that's caked all over my face and hands. I hesitate, and she grips my arm tight to her side.

"Reverend Frye." Your voice startles me.

The preacher looks up at the platform as if dazed.

"Miss Finch and I will be at the church tomorrow morning, ready for you to marry us."

Mother's jaw drops. Darrel flings his hat into the air. Eunice Robinson pushes through the crowd toward her house, followed by her sisters. Maria's dark eyes are full of laughter as she leads me down the stairs.

Now

I.

Maria insists I wear her china-blue wedding dress.

She has trimmed and brushed and combed me, and braided plaits interwoven with dried flowers, just like she wore on her wedding day. She arranged a triangle of lace as my bridal cap and told me I look lovely.

For your sake I hope so.

Somehow I ate and bathed and slept and rose and dressed.

I must have, for here I am now, ready to walk to my wedding.

II.

Maria goes inside for her shawl, and Leon speaks to me. It's not easy for him.

"Did Lottie suffer long, Miss Finch?"

"Oh," I say. I look away.

He leans toward me, pleading with me to look at him. "I swear to you, if I'd ever dreamed . . ."

Leon Cartwright. I feel awkward for Maria. Poor Lottie. But to be her young beau, and then to have wondered what happened, all these years, and grieve?

"Nott for very long, Mr. Cartwrightt."

His eyes grow red. "I would have married her," he says "We were both so young."

I nod. Young love is not always forever. I know.

Maria appears in the doorway, beaming at us. I watch Leon gaze at his wife.

"Thank you for wishing me joy," I tell Leon as Maria draws near. He nods.

III.

We arrive at the church early. I don't want to be led there by a parade of villagers, if any would care to come. I want to sit quietly and think. Maria holds my hands and chatters at me.

The door opens. You come into the chapel, brushed and shaven and pressed.

Maria slips away, murmuring about something she forgot at home.

You sit beside me, gingerly, as though I might break if you touched me. You look at me. I look back into your beautiful bruised face, at the morning illuminating your green eyes. I can't read them.

"What'ss the matter?" I ask, pulling back.

"Nothing," you say. You take my hands and kiss my fingertips. Yet you look so serious that I begin to worry.

The empty church is silent and bright. There are only the two of us, breathing together. You trace your finger across my forehead, down my nose, and onto my lips. I watch your eyes as they follow your finger's path along my skin.

Your words are a whisper. "Are you truly here? And truly mine?"

I hope my eyes are answer enough. Just in case, though, I catch your finger between my teeth, and bite.

Your laughter rings off the ceiling beams. Bruises can't

stop your eyes from flashing wickedly. "Run away west with me, Judith. Right now. Phantom's outside. What do you say?"

"All rightt," I say. "We're nott dressed for it, though."

"True." You pluck at your black coat, then finger my lace cap. "Since we're here, we might as well get married."

I shrug. "If you inssistt."

You kiss my fingertips once more and return the bite. "I do insist."

You offer me your arm and squeeze mine tight. We rise and walk up the same aisle that they dragged us down the day before.

Reverend Frye stumps his way up the aisle. Elizabeth follows, carrying his robes, and she smiles shyly at me. I hear a noise at the rear of the church. I turn to see the doors open. Darrel comes in, arm in arm with Goody Pruett. He waves his hat at me. Maria and Leon are back, too. They are all so dear to me now. This day swallows them up in love.

Reverend Frye keeps it brief.

And then you are mine.

IV.

Phantom pulls us home in the cart. Even she is braided and beribboned for the marriage. Fortunately she can drive us home without needing our help. Our attention is not on the reins.

Will we stay here? Will we journey on? Today is not a day for answering such questions.

On the step of your home—our home—we find baskets of food and jars of preserves.

Trying to eat them is your mule.

And there is a box. A wooden trunk with FINCH branded on one side. It was my father's.

Inside are sheets and towels and a quilt, all bearing my mother's fine stitching. I caress the smooth, soft fabrics.

This box is full of words my mother can't bring herself to say.

We drag the box inside, and lock the door.

Acknowledgments

A fount of blessings made *All the Truth That's in Me* possible. I'm grateful to Vermont College of the Fine Arts for creating an atmosphere that fostered and demanded my best work. Sarah Aronson, Jill Santopolo, Gwenda Bond, and Rita Williams-Garcia's early enthusiasm for this piece gave me much-needed hope. And Tim Wynne-Jones mentored the project from start to finish with his trademark generosity, wisdom, and warmth. I love him.

Blessing spilled over beyond VCFA's Montpelier campus. My agent, Alyssa Eisner Henkin, championed this project in all the right ways. My editor, Kendra Levin, took over where Tim left off, lovingly and astutely showing me what the novel yet lacked. She made our collaboration a delight. Her colleagues at Penguin Young Readers Group linked arms and surrounded this project with support. Regina Hayes, Ken Wright, Janet Pascal, Vanessa Han, Eileen Savage, Kim Ryan, Jennifer Loja, Don Weisberg, the marketing team, and the sales force, thank you for your diligent efforts, and for your faith in Judith's story.

Where public thanks are owed the most, I'm left unsure of how to offer them. There comes a time, when we write, if we're lucky, when we recognize that grace involved itself in our work, and we are not entirely in charge of things. This was such a project, and I am such a debtor; I claim any faults as my own.

I try to write for the world, but in truth there's just one reader I dearly hope to please. This book is for him. On some level every love story I write is my attempt to show the world what Phil means to me. Someday, I pray, I'll get it right.